AVA

BY HANNAH HOFFMEISTER

BOOK 1 IN THE DREAM RING SERIES

*To Pat —
Enjoy!
Hannah L.
Hoffmeister*

© Buttonwood Press 2011

This novel is a product of the author's imagination. The events described in this story never occurred. Though localities, buildings, and businesses may exist, liberties were taken with their actual location and description. This story has no purpose other than to entertain the reader.

Published by Buttonwood Press
P.O. Box 716
Haslett, Michigan 48840
www.buttonwoodpress.com

ISBN: 987-0-9823351-5-4
Printed in the United States of America

I dedicate this book to my 7th grade class.
Although we were a difficult class,
I will always remember a cherished year
full of great personalities and fun.

I also dedicate this book to
Sarah "Cassandra" Sax, who was
my childhood playmate and is my forever
friend! We have lots of great memories,
and I really appreciate her help with
<u>Ava: Book 1 in the Dream Ring Series</u>.

ABOUT THE AUTHOR

www.dreamringseries.com

Hannah Hoffmeister is thirteen years old and lives in St. Louis, Missouri. This is her first published novel. When she's not writing the Dream Ring Series, she is hanging out with friends, playing softball, cheering on the St. Louis Cardinals, gardening, or reading.

ACKNOWLEDGEMENTS

I would like to thank so many people for helping me with Ava: Book 1 in the Dream Ring Series. First, I would like to thank my mom; she's always been very supportive of my characters and plots and has been a great editor. I would also like to thank my dad, who waited so patiently until he was allowed to read it and gave great ideas and a helpful review. Thank you to Grandpa Baldwin, who has never left my side in my development as an author, and Nana, who is a great role model and someone whose opinion I value and trust.

Thank you to my publisher, Buttonwood Press, and their highly talented staff: Editor, Anne Ordiway; Proofreader, Joyce Wagner; and Cover Designer and Typesetter, Sarah Thomas. Thanks to my large extended family for all of your love and encouragement! Thank you Mrs. Renkins and Tagen, for your wonderful endorsements! I would like to thank my friends for providing ideas, inspiration, and lots of support. Thanks to my brother Louis and my sister Norah for writing your own books after hearing about mine. ☺ And last but not least, I absolutely have to thank my brother Tom for his advice, ideas, quotes, and listening ear!

Chapter One

Birthdays rock. *Thirteenth* birthdays are even better!

I tell you, I woke up on the morning of my thirteenth birthday in the best mood, ready to test my teenage limits to the fullest and bother everyone with my annoying attitude. It would be sweet.

Now, if I had known then what I know now, it would be a different story. But that's what makes it so good.

Anyway, I stretched, got out of bed, and put on a light yellow tank top and jean shorts. My legs were still a sickly pale color, but they would tan as summer came. The pool is Ava's reign!

"Ava!" my mom said, coming into my room as I was turning my phone on and unplugging it from its charger. I got about a million texts from my friends wishing me a happy birthday. I smiled, applied chap-stick, and turned to face my mother.

Lilly Popolis wore a maroon skirt, a white blouse, maroon earrings, maroon heels, and—you guessed it—a maroon headband. She was grinning, her lips coated in a sheen of maroon lipstick. And her toenails and fingernails were done in maroon polish. Gosh, what overkill.

"Mom," I said, examining her outfit. "You look… maroon."

That was really the only way to describe it—it was gross. No one looks good in that much of one color.

"Thank you, dear," she said, clapping her hands and giving me a birthday hug. "You know I display my moods in a colorful way. To me, maroon means happiness, and I am wearing the happiness that my baby is thirteen. Happy birthday, sweetie."

I rolled my eyes and hugged her back, then began brushing my blond hair back into a ponytail.

"Breakfast is ready," she said. "Come downstairs for some pancakes, and then we'll do whatever you want. How does that sound to my little teenager?"

Little and *teenager* do not make a good phrase, but I was in too good of a mood to argue, so I said, "Yum," and followed her downstairs. A steaming plate of pancakes waited in a kitchen full of streamers and balloons covered with the number "13" and two exclamation marks after it. I sat down and began shoveling in the fluffy pancakes with sugar and syrup on top in a wave of buttery goodness. Amen.

Dad came into the kitchen and gave me a big hug. Malcolm Popolis was a big, muscular man with kind eyes and a heart bigger than anyone I'd ever known. He gave me a kiss on the cheek, sang "Happy Birthday" to me in a deep, throaty voice, grabbed his briefcase, gave Mom a kiss, and left for work.

"I think we should go shopping," I declared between bites.

"Does Victoria want to come?" she asked, referring to my best friend in the entire universe.

"Probably not. She's really into this science experiment, and she most likely won't want to stop working on it."

"Okay," she said, smiling. "Get in the car when you're finished and we'll head to the mall."

"Cool." I reached into the clay bowl the keys were always kept in and tossed them to Mom. I hurriedly finished my breakfast and gave my dog a kiss. Then, after slipping on my new flip-flops, I ran out the door. *Go* and *shopping* put together make the best phrase in the world!

⟶⟵ ❋ ⟶⟵

After the mall (and Mom) had lavishly supplied me with perfume, a new skirt—perfect for the pool parties Victoria and I had planned, tank tops, and an awesome magazine, we went home, sipping Sprite as we exited the highway. I'd had a great day, but I really wanted to see Vic now. She would love my new skirt; Mom had let me get one for her, too, in different colors, of course.

I hopped out of the car and skipped along the sidewalk to Victoria's house. She only lived a few houses down, and I have practically worn a trail into the sidewalk over the years; I went there *that* often. I came upon a patch of dirt where there was no sidewalk block. Apparently someone was getting a new block put in, and the hole was dirty, a little muddy, and totally gross. I walked on my tip-toes, trying not to get my new flip-flops dirty. The hole was nasty, and it hadn't been there yesterday.

And then the weirdest thing happened. It still creeps me out.

I began falling. Like, the ground just sunk and disappeared and—*whoosh*—I was just falling, falling, falling. It felt like a long way—and it was dark—and then I landed on soft foam. Several men in purple robes—and it was as odd as it sounds— were standing around me, staring at me curiously. I stifled a scream and looked back at them. They had old, wise faces, and were looking at me, like I said, curiously. They began shaking my hand and saying, "Ava, Ava, happy birthday!" By then I was convinced I was crazy. I pinched myself to see if I could, like, transport myself back to the sidewalk square—*above ground, that is*—and get this—it worked! I was again standing on top of the empty sidewalk space. My arms began to shake, and my hands felt clammy.

There was no way I could go to Victoria's now. Too many freaky things had happened lately. I turned back towards my house, surprised to see the shopping bag still in my hand. It hadn't been in my hand when I was underground. Weird.

I sprinted home and ran through our hall until I got to Mom's bedroom. She was watching TV while she exercised on the treadmill, like everything was fine, like I hadn't just had the worst, freakiest experience I had ever gone through, like everything was still the same.

I guess she saw the wild look in my eye; she immediately turned off the treadmill and asked why I was shaking like a leaf.

"I—I—I don't know," I admitted. "Mom, a lot of strange things have been happening to me lately. Like, at the bus stop, these men came up to me, all dressed in purple… robes, I guess they were. They each shook my hand and said, 'Ava Popolis. How nice to meet you. I am interested to find out your powers. Your mother was always such a nice person.' Like, how weird is that? I bet they were on a *lot* of drugs."

Mom just looked amused.

"And then, the other day, I was at the movies with Victoria, you know? And the ticket lady said, 'Ava. Weather, fingernails, and unknown. Victoria. Ice, flowers, and unknown.' *What* was she *talking* about?"

Mom looked a little more amused, and her fingernails were turning darker maroon every minute. For some reason that didn't strike me as weird at the time.

"And then, just a couple of days ago… well, I was in Wal-Mart, shopping for my half of the grocery list while you were on the other side of the store. And this woman came up to me. She swapped my half-filled cart for a full one. And get this: it had *everything* I needed, nothing more, nothing less. And then, one minute she was there, the next minute, gone."

Mom shook her head. "This is bad. People using magic in plain sight. I'm going to have to write a letter," she muttered.

"*What?!* Mom, talk in *English* please. That's what we *speak*. Anyway, I headed to Victoria's today and I fell in this hole that wasn't really a hole. Really strange. And these weird guys, looking kinda like the dudes at the bus stop, shook my hand. And... what... was... that!?" I screeched, feeling almost hysterical now. I had kept the encounters with these weird people to myself for a while because they'd only worry Mom and I hadn't been harmed. Besides, I'm thirteen, and I deal with strange people every day!

Mom got a strange glint in her eyes, most definitely amused.

"Mom!"

"Honey, come with me," she said, looking around to see if anyone could see us.

Chapter Two

"Mom, what just happened to me?" I asked again. We were in my room, and she had pulled the curtains down and locked my door. Now we were under the blankets of my bottom bunk with a flashlight.

"Are you sure no one's outside?" she asked for about the hundredth time.

"Yes, Mom! Now, what's going on!? Why are we having this 'life-changing conversation' under these stuffy covers? This is just a *little* awkward." I pushed the blankets off us, and Mom—thankfully—didn't object.

"Oh, yes, of course. Well, Ava, you just had a meeting with the People."

"Mom, you've mentioned that maybe a *few* times," I said sarcastically. Who are 'The People?'"

"Well, you see, you were born one of them."

"One of who?!"

"The witches."

"No way. I am *not* a witch." I took a deep breath. "I haven't been *that* moody lately."

"Yes you are. And that's not the reason that I'm saying this," Mom said.

"Are you okay?" I asked.

"Of course. I'll tell you the story: When Grandma turned thirteen," she started, "she had powers. We don't know why it started for our family in her generation, but it did. A mysterious letter beckoned her to the witch world. There she met your grandpa at the school." Her eyes got all starry—these were her parents we were talking about. "When they had me, since Grandpa and Grandma were both magical (Grandma was a witch, Grandpa, a wizard), I was born purely a witch. But, since I married a mortal, when we had you, you are half-witch."

"I'm *normal!*" I insisted, my voice getting shrill and high, my breath growing short and fast.

"Just let me finish," Mom said. "When a special one like you turns thirteen, the parents of the child must inform him or her of the situation. They *must*. There's one exception, though. If you are born purely a witch, your parents can tell you earlier if they wish."

"So, uh, since I'm a *witch*," (I half-shuddered, half-laughed at the thought, since it was surely a joke), "do I have powers? I mean, what do I *do?*"

"Well, of course you have powers, but they aren't developed yet. You are going to have Fingernails, though, like me."

"I already have fingernails." What was *up* with her?

"Yes, but the *power* Fingernails."

"Why?"

"Because *I* have that power."

"You do? What does that even *mean*? Mom, are you *sure* you're okay?"

"Yes, honey. But I'll explain later."

"Is Victoria a witch?" I asked, hoping that one of my friends was at least *half*-witch—*if* she was serious.

"I believe so."

"Can I talk to her about this?" I asked hopefully.

"Oh, no, you must not!" Mom said forcefully. "In the future, dear, but not yet."

"So, will I go to 'witch world' or something?" I laughed. Mom glared at me, like *Young missy, this is not a joke.*

"Yes, of course. At the end of the summer."

"Good one, Mom."

"Ava, I'm truly serious."

"Whoa..." I was overwhelmed, starting to think that maybe Mom *wasn't* joking. She'd never kept up a practical joke with me *this* long.

"Well, I guess I'll give you some time to digest what I told ya. I'll be making dinner. Okay?"

"Yep." I nodded, then cradled my head in my hands, feeling a bit dizzy.

As soon as the door closed, I flopped onto the bed and groaned loudly. Why did I have to be a witch? Why couldn't I just be a normal teenager with regular teenage problems? Now, on top of everything teens have to learn, I had to be a... witch. Oh, this was not good. I've only *been* a teenager for, like, less than twenty-four hours, and I've already had this "life-changing experience." What else could possibly happen?

Chapter Three

"Now, the school for witches is on Neptune, so you'll have to fly there," Mom said seriously. I was glad to have almost the entire summer before I had to join the freak show bandwagon, but I would still miss eighth grade at school, which everyone knew was the best year. Now I had to learn to do magic instead.

"But aren't plane tickets expensive?" I asked. I forgot that we were going to another planet!

"No, silly! You're flying there on your broom. And let me explain to you a little bit about the People, since that info. was missing when we had our conversation a few months ago. The People are a group of wizards designated to inform the young teenagers of their ancestry. Their mission is to sort of spur that conversation on, and they have very accurate records of the millions of teenage witches and wizards around the world. They present the information in different ways, of course. And they are *not* on drugs, as you so offensively suggested on your thirteenth birthday."

"Ohhhh-kay. Yeah, whatever. I don't have a broom. And besides, they're only good for sweeping."

Mom ignored my last comment. "You do now... it's your birthday present from me."

"Thanks. I think."

"Victoria's mother, Maureen, told me that she has informed Victoria. We were old school buddies on Neptune, and I just wasn't sure when she would tell Victoria. It's free game. Chat about it all you want."

"Okay, well, I'm gonna head over there. Victoria and I need to have a serious conversation. I'll call you around lunchtime."

"Bye."

"TTYL."

Ding-dong. The doorbell rang, loud and clear, at Victoria's.

"Hello, Ava! Victoria is up in her room doing homework. Would you take this apple up to her? She's been working on a science project and didn't come down for breakfast."

"Will do. Thanks, Mrs. Mongrelo."

"Hey, how's your science project going?" I asked as I walked in. Victoria always does projects during the summer, because our school offers extra credit for them when we return from summer break. Now that I think about it, Victoria shouldn't have done the science project because the school on Neptune most likely didn't offer extra credit for dedicated students.

Victoria's room is turquoise and brown, and it has a great, calming vibe just emanating from the walls. It's my favorite place to hang out in the summer. I sat down in her butterfly chair and propped my feet on her ottoman. I already felt more relaxed.

"Great." Victoria absently pushed back her long, brown hair and bent over to record something.

"What's it on?" I flopped on her bed and sighed.

"Actually, I was going to do it on 'magic,' but now I've decided to do it on which brand of markers stay juiced up the longest. It's kinda boring."

"Oh. Your mom wanted me to bring this to you." I handed her the apple.

"Thanks."

I decided to bring up the witch situation first. "What do you think about the whole 'witch' thing?"

"Strangely, I think it's interesting," she said, grinning.

"Weren't you surprised?" I asked.

"Not as much as you, I bet. You see, my mom isn't really a good 'hider' of things. She's been acting strange, going out a lot. I thought it was a surprise for me or something. But Mom always tells me stuff, so I let it go until she told me. Your parents know how to hide things, though."

"Is your dad a wizard?"

"Nope. I'm only half-witch."

"So am I! Twins!" Laughing, we did our handshake we always do when something is the same. That actually made our situation seem less odd, almost normal, since we were in it together now.

"So, I guess we're going to the school pretty soon," I said absently, twirling my hair around on my finger.

"Yeah." Victoria munched on her apple thoughtfully, and I almost laughed at the serious expression on her face.

"Do you have a 'mobile' yet? Like, a broom or whatever?" I asked.

"No, Mom said I'll ride on yours for the first year, if it's cool with you. If I save up the money, she'll let me buy one. I wonder if anything will be different there. What do you think?"

"I think *everything* will be different there! We'll ride on *brooms*. Brooms! And if that's not odd enough, we have to have powers and learn magic! I don't know if I'll ever get used to the idea of being a witch!" I paused to let my dramatic monologue sink in. "Are you going to be a good witch or a bad witch?" I asked with a grin.

"A good one, of course! A *stylish* witch with *attitude!*" Victoria laughed, and threw the apple core in her trash can.

"Me too!" All of a sudden, I felt a zap—kinda like an electric shock—go through my body and I heard myself saying, "Please get my mom." Then I fell back on Victoria's bed into a deep sleep. That was when I had my first encounter with Widdidorm.

Chapter Four

"You have your toothbrush, your clothes, your supplies on the list, your hairbrush, and the manual to your broom?" Mom asked, one week after I had talked to Victoria. It was now almost the middle of August, and my school on Earth was starting next week. We were leaving today, and I felt nervous and strange.

"Yes, Mom, I've got everything. I'll call if I forgot anything and you can bring it up when you visit me."

"How many times have I told you that you can't *call* people on another planet?" She finally sounded annoyed with me, which was understandable. She was probably bothered by my continued skepticism and denial that this thing was real—that *would* be kind of insulting, I guess—my resistance to going to this school, and—what else?—my attitude.

"Fine. I'll text you, then."

"No, you'll send a letter with your messenger."

"I don't *have* a messenger. I know, I'll just use my finger and—bippity, boppity, boo!—you'll get my message!" I waved an imaginary wand around in the air for emphasis.

Mom ignored my comment, which I got quite a hoot out of. "You'll understand soon. It's the way you get mail. *My* messenger is purple with two black streaks and one orange eye. Her name is Bunny."

"Sure. Okay, Mom."

"All right, let's go," she said, and opened the garage door. I had already said goodbye to Dad earlier this morning, when he had left for work. Mom had told me that she had convinced him that I had been accepted to a student exchange program, and would be spending the next school year at a boarding school in rural Europe. He had given me a tender hug and a promise to write, and I knew I would miss him dearly. How we would communicate was still sort of an enigma to me, since he did *not* have a messenger, most definitely. The fact that he had been married to Mom all this time and *still* didn't know we were a different type of person was very puzzling to me. I just hoped I wouldn't slip up in my letters and say something like, "Yeah, Dad, and I've been having a great time changing a piece of paper into a unicorn. How about your life?"

I kissed my dog, Goldie, one more time, and headed out to the car.

As I left, I passed the silver frame containing a photo taken at Victoria's birthday party. There I was, my gold, wavy hair tied back in a ponytail; I had obviously tried to corral the frizzy locks, but without much luck. My blue eyes shone brightly, even in the picture. Victoria was a little taller than I was, and her hair was long and brown, pulled up in a pretty French braid, while mine was shoulder-length, high up in a ponytail. Her eyes were bright with happiness, sparkling like emeralds. Her cheeks were rosy, accenting her high cheekbones and perfect, naturally tan skin. We had our arms around each other, both smiling at the camera. That had been one of the best sleepovers in our BFF history. Now we were beginning something new for our history—witch-dom.

When we reached the park from which we would leave, I noticed that several brooms were spread out on the ground. Mom pointed mine out to me. "Go ahead and put your stuff in your broom's cellar, then sit up here while you wait for further instructions. You can talk to one of the teachers if something happens. You'll take breaks every few hours or so on your trip. You'll sleep in your cellar for the night, and then you'll be there."

"Great. I'll see you at the end of the first semester." I hugged my mom just as Victoria arrived, acting tough instead of like a scared coward, which was how I really felt.

"Five minutes until we leave!" a voice blared over a seemingly invisible loudspeaker. "We suggest you go to the bathroom!"

After we put my stuff in the "cellar" of my broom (which was really just a little invisible carrying space underneath the broom), Victoria and I went to the bathroom, then bought three packs of Skittles and two bottles of Diet Coke. We looked at each other, wondering what would happen on the other planet.

We were headed for Neptune. Neptune! Since it was so far away, I guessed that our trip would be magically shortened, or sped up in some fashion. This witch stuff might actually come in handy! Never mind, scratch that. Witch-dom was just *strange*.

My broom looked like an ordinary broom, a wooden stick with plastic bristles on the end. It was smooth and sleek, though, definitely brand-new.

"For any of you who don't know, you do not *straddle* your broom. That is only in movies. For this trip, you will sit sideways on your brooms, like riding sidesaddle, okay? And *don't fall off*!"

"Please board your brooms," the voice over the loudspeaker continued. Then the loudspeaker commanded, "Hover," and the broom snapped to attention in my hands. I got on, "sidesaddle," as the booming voice continued, "Please say bye to your folks, because we are taking off in, 10, 9, 8, 7, 6, 5, 4, 3, 2, 1!"

Then she (it was definitely a female voice) said, "Oomba!" *(Oomba?!?)* And all of a sudden, we were lifted off the ground, moving upward. We—at least I did—felt like we were suspended in air; the freak show became a marionette puppet play. At first I felt like I was going to slide right off the broomstick, but some charm must have been put on it to make sure that I didn't. Victoria and I didn't have time to either laugh at the freeing feeling of the broom-ride or cry at the thought of going to another planet alone. We just looked at each other and clenched our hands tighter on the broom handle.

"We need to turn!" Vic screeched. I stuck my hand into the freezing wind and pointed to the right, hoping maybe that would turn us. Sure enough, it worked. I didn't have time to think about how cool and frightening that was all at once. I looked at her, and our faces mirrored our fear and excitement. This was turning into more of an adventure than I had imagined. At least we were together.

I looked back at the earth after we had been flying about fifteen minutes. It shrank in size every second, and I was super-scared to be floating away from my anchor. I gasped, realizing how high we were off the ground—with nothing stopping us if we were to fall—and quickly turned my gaze back to the broom handle. My fear of heights increased by the moment after that view of Earth. It was beautiful, but, hey, I wasn't on a scenic tour! My goal was to stay on the broom and not fall off.

After a couple of hours of flying, I was finally used to the wooden, solid feeling of my broom and the endless drop below.

"Break in ten minutes," the mysterious voice said an hour later, loud enough for the entire freshman year to hear it. "Bring money; this is the lunch stop."

When we reached the stop, I pressed a button that indicated "Reverse" and parked. (How I had any idea how to *fly* a *broom*— or *park* it—I have no clue. I think mostly I was guessing!)

We parked our brooms next to a big gray space station without walls—it was just a floating floor. Weird. *Very* weird.

The cafeteria part had small red and orange circular tables scattered around the gray floor and two bathrooms down a narrow walkway.

"Here we are!" I sang merrily as I set my black and white purse down. But suddenly, I felt a sleepy sensation. I fought it, and stayed awake long enough to tell Victoria I felt extremely sleepy. She said I was air-sick, but I doubted it. I had had this feeling before, on Earth. This was no sudden nap; more like a message (through sleep) that I didn't want. Am I being called again by Widdidorm? What could he *possibly* want?

"I'll get someone! Try to stay awake!" Victoria yelled frantically. I was a bit scared; what if this happened while we were flying, and I fell off my broom? After a few seconds, I fell fast asleep. I slumped down on the table I had been sitting at. The entire freshman class of this school probably thought I was a slob who was really tired and rude enough to exemplify that in front of everybody. How embarrassing!

"Ava! Ava! Earth to Ava! Wake up already! We're going to leave soon! Ava? You all right?" Victoria was shaking me awake. "Ava! We're at the station. Remember, we're going to Neptune to learn powers and magic?"

"Oh. Yeah." I felt bleary-eyed and momentarily confused. Even odder things were happening to me in space than on Earth.

I went to the bathroom (thankfully, it did have walls), which was shiny and futuristic-looking—all stainless steel and polished metal—then ordered a to-go lunch at the concession stand and headed back to my broom, feeling normal. There had been a couple times on this trip I have kind of wished I wasn't so "special" after all.

We reached the next stop with no trouble. Thankfully, I didn't fall asleep this time.

"We are approaching the Asteroid Belt," the voice said. "Please! I suggest that *everybody* go to the bathroom before we return to our mobiles." Everyone made a beeline for the bathrooms, and seven more stalls appeared.

The Asteroid Belt was hard to navigate; Victoria and I made most of the turns at the last minute, but we came out okay. The only injuries in the freshman class were a couple of bruises. The asteroids that had skimmed us were just little rocks — nothing bigger, thankfully.

"One more day 'til we reach Neptune!" the voice said. "Please press the red button that says 'Automatic' and go to bed!" Victoria pushed the button and headed for the cellar, and I followed.

Our tiny little cellar had magically expanded about nine times the size it was last time I saw it. It had now transformed into a bedroom with sea-foam green painted walls, a chair, and twin beds. We stashed our bags in a compartment by our beds. Then a sink appeared and we brushed our teeth.

"Isn't this fun?" Victoria whispered from her twin bed.

"Maybe it is for you; *you* never get sucked into some dark, scary world without any warning," I said a bit irritably.

"Maybe someone on Neptune knows what happened," she said, totally ignoring the fact that I had just completely confided in her about what was happening to me when I 'fell asleep.' "'Night."

"'Night."

When I woke, we were entering the atmosphere of Neptune. After changing into robes, sweatpants, and a t-shirt, I emerged from the cellar and took a look around. I couldn't believe how different it was from Earth—there were beautiful colors swirling around, and a light rain was falling, refreshing the hundreds of groggy teenagers sitting on brooms. Hues of green and turquoise and aqua surrounded the big planet, obscuring our view of the actual land. I patted my hair and was disgusted to feel the blond locks expanding into frizzy puffs. I put on a baseball hat and cringed. So *not* how I wanted to enter the second planet I've ever been on!

Since Neptune is so far from the sun, the weather is always chilly. I learned that the hard way. For our arrival, I wore a pink tank top with sequins and a jean skirt that made my legs look long and graceful. My flip-flops matched the tank top, and I sported fake diamond earrings. Although the hat did kind of cramp the style, it was necessary, and I had to accept that. But I got serious goose bumps the minute we entered the atmosphere, so I quickly changed in the cellar into something more appropriate: jeans and a sweatshirt. Not as stylish, but so much warmer!

Chapter Five

"WE'RE HERE!" I shouted excitedly. I looked at the sign above the grand entrance: *Dream Ring.* Mom said I'd be surprised when I learned what the school was called. I'd begged her to tell me, but she'd kept her mouth closed.

"Dream Ring! Isn't that the prettiest name for a school?" I asked Victoria.

"Yes," Victoria said, looking at the building delightedly. The building took my breath away—it was a castle made of stone. The stone was beautifully shiny and polished, as if it was brand-new, even though I was pretty sure it was at least three hundred years old. The school had three big towers, and the most elegant doors you have ever seen. We're talking, like, well-kept, medieval-looking buildings here.

The main hall was the prettiest of all. Its stone was different, just… shinier, I guess. And something about the way it was constructed made it look like it should be the center of attention.

It had white marble columns and steps leading up to gigantic oak doors.

And then there was Neptune itself. Although the light wasn't as bright as Earth's, the land was absolutely brilliant here and covered in all the colors of the rainbow. The leaves were a fiery red and the little birds flitting in the nearby trees were pale orange. Yellow sunlight, emerald green grass, a bright blue sky, and flowers of deep purple bordered the main hall. The weather was cold, but that didn't make the landscape any dimmer. Swirling clouds of gas surrounded the planet, and there were narrow rings farther away that were very icy and thin. There was lush green grass on the campus, with nice big trees. They had big, waxy leaves, as big as an elephant's ear, unlike anything I'd ever seen; I guess the leaves were extra big to help them soak up more sunlight.

The air we were breathing didn't give any other result than Earth, so I figured that—since we were witches—we could breathe whatever strange gases were on Neptune. I didn't feel any different, or deprived of oxygen or anything, so I wasn't sure what had happened. I would have to ask one of the teachers when we started classes. I nudged Victoria and took a dramatic breath, and then smiled. She got the message without words, and I knew that we were both relieved that the air didn't feel any different than Earth.

I'd heard that there was a big ocean somewhere on Neptune, and a chain of mountains, too. All I had seen so far of this beautiful planet was the campus, and I was highly impressed.

I had expected, like, a gray landscape with gray buildings and barely any sunlight. This magical place—literally *magical*—was just the opposite.

"Hello, students! My name is Licklici,"—she pronounced it lick-liss-ee—"and I am your headmistress! Welcome, I am so very excited you made it! Come on in, come on in," she said. She was very pretty, a sweet blonde, in flowing golden robes with a white dress underneath. Her big hoop earrings matched her outfit perfectly and dainty white slippers peeked from under her long dress.

"Is this your first year?" she asked us as we walked up the steps, probably knowing the answer but asking us anyway.

"Yes!" we all said. There were probably about 180 of us. Hey, strength in numbers.

"Then please meet my elf, Cowcatine. He'll be your greeter for the next four years. Cowcatine, these are the new first-year students!" She smiled.

"Hello," Cowcatine said, grinning. "Welcome to Dream Ring." Cowcatine was pudgy and friendly-looking, wearing a purple outfit that accentuated his round, squishy middle. Life as a greeter must not be an active existence. *Dude, if you would take a lap around the castle, the outfit might fit you better*, I thought. His eyes were kind, though, and he gave us a big, compassionate smile when it was our turn to shake his hand.

"Nice to meet you, Cowcatine," Victoria and I said.

"My, you are pretty. Welcome," Cowcatine said in a voice that sounded very un-human, squeaky and alien-ish. We laughed and walked away.

"He is so hilarious!" I said through my fit of laughter. Victoria laughed hysterically, too. I was so lucky to have her next to me. I would die if I didn't!

We walked into the main hall, where we would eat on fancy occasions. It was almost time for the opening dinner, but the long tables were empty, and I couldn't smell any food. Believe me, flying kicks up hunger from the pit of your stomach, and I was beyond ready to smell some food.

"Where's the food?" I asked Victoria.

"I dunno, do you see any?" Victoria whispered.

"No," I whispered back.

"Now, a headset will be at your place and your name will be floating above," Licklici said as we walked in. "Your table is over there." She pointed us to the far right corner. "That's where you will eat on holidays or special occasions," she told us.

The name cards were awesome. Our names were written on them in a fancy scroll, and mini-lights surrounded the letters. Some of the lights blinked, some of the lights flashed, and others just did what they wanted. It seemed like they had minds of their own! A faint buzzing came from the name cards, and probably the headset too, as if they were working hard to keep themselves in the air.

The headsets were all different colors; mine was blue, and Vic's was lime green. They looked kind of like magic earmuffs.

The main hall was a deep violet. Our tables were surrounded by mini-lights, which upon closer view turned out to be small pixies. They smiled and whispered welcome to us, which kind of freaked me out!

We headed over to our new table and found our places. Victoria and I were seated right next to each other. Two boys who had talked the whole way to Dream Ring were sitting next to each other also. The more I thought about it, though, it was probably magic.

"Hi, what's your name?" I asked a girl on the left of me; she had curly brown hair and gold hoops on her ears.

"I'm Kathryn," she said in a very high voice. "Kathryn Aden."

"I'm Ava," I said. "So, this is your first year?"

"Yep," she said. "Isn't this place huge?"

"Totally!" I exclaimed. *And a little overwhelming,* I thought.

"So, what group do you wanna be in?" she asked.

"Huh?" I asked, confused. What was she talking about?

"The groups," she repeated. "Don't you know?"

Gee, right when I'm about to make a friend, I have to go and be stupid.

"I'll explain," she sighed. Under her curly bangs, it almost looked like she rolled her eyes.

"See, everyone gets put in a group. You can be in Yurnia or Talania. I want to be in Yurnia. Everyone says that the smart ones are always in Yurnia, and the dumb ones go into Talania. We'll be assigned to our groups after dinner."

This was something totally new. I couldn't believe Mom didn't tell me about this!

"Please put on your headsets," a voice over a megaphone shouted. But I soon found out that it wasn't a megaphone. It was a person with a regular human voice—with a spell on it.

Chapter Six

"Attention, please!" the person with the magnified voice boomed. "Everyone needs to put on their headsets. If you don't, dinner won't come to you, so it is extremely important that you follow my instructions." I looked toward the source of the voice again. It came from a short, fat woman with a million diamonds twinkling all over her robes. I wondered how important you had to be to have that many diamonds.

Victoria, Kathryn, and I put on our headsets, just snapping the earmuffs onto our heads. They fit perfectly! The boys who were always talking and disobeying the rules had actually put on their headsets, too.

"Now, I want you all to think about dinnerware. A plate, knife, spoon, fork, and glass. If you think hard enough, they will come to you." That made no sense, but I wished it anyway.

I wished with all my might, and a plate, knife, spoon, fork, and glass appeared on the table in front of me. I jumped back and stared at them, then touched the plate tentatively with my finger to see if it was actually *there*. It was.

I looked around. The others must have not been as focused as me, because most of them didn't have silverware; haha! Suddenly, Victoria's plate appeared. She pumped her arm into the air and knocked me in the head.

"I finally did it!" she whispered excitedly. She looked at the boys. They were frowning because nothing was in front of them. Maybe they wouldn't get dinner. The thought made me laugh.

"Now, I want you all to think about food. Any kind of food, but make sure it's something you like," the voice continued. "If you wish hard enough, that dish will appear in front of you. Proceed."

"I wish, I wish that I had some of Mom's good fried chicken with garlic mashed potatoes, and fresh cucumbers, with a glass of milk. I wish, I wish, I wish." Suddenly, a plate of fried chicken, garlic mashed potatoes, fresh cucumber slices, and a glass of milk appeared in front of me. I said a quick prayer, and dug in. The others stared at me. They had no food in front of them yet.

"Mmm, this is so good, I wish I could have more," I thought silently after I had cleaned off my plate. *"I wish, I wish, I wish."* More food appeared in front of me. By now, the others had their first helping; I was done before them. The food was so good, and it reminded me of home.

But the boys were hilarious. They couldn't focus hard enough to get silverware, so they ate with their fingers! And one boy, Josh, didn't even get food. We all giggled at our table as

Josh sat through the whole dinner, eyes squinted, wishing for his supper.

"Now, when you're done, people in their first year should come over to the room in the far left corner," the voice boomed. I wished that my plate was cleaned and would disappear; a soapy dishrag and a jug of water appeared, cleaned my dinnerware for me, and then disappeared without wetting the tablecloth. After slipping off my earmuffs, I hurried to the far left corner before I could notice the stares that followed me.

"Okay, you can come in now," a male voice said. I jumped; he had startled me. I took a deep breath and walked inside.

It was very, very dark in the room. I assumed the man in the corner was the one with the voice that had startled me. He held a lit candle in one hand and a feather in his other hand. By his candle, I could see that the floor was just soil. I was glad that I was wearing shoes, because the floor would have totally ruined my pedicure. (Okay, so I have my girly-girl moments—who doesn't? And that pedicure had been a rare gem; something I almost never received from my "thrifty" mom.)

I was the only one in the room, and everyone else was still at dinner. But as the students finished, they lined up at the entrance to the corner room.

"Come over here," the man said in his spooky, weird voice. I hesitated, and then walked over to where he sat on a stool. His accent was something European, I thought, but I couldn't quite tell.

"Now," he said, "This feather is going to tell me which group you belong in. On the count of three, Natasha, (he pointed to the corner, where a freakishly skinny woman with a candle and a fan was almost lost in the darkness), will turn the fan, and the feather will say which group you will be in."

"Sure, okay, go ahead," I said a bit nervously, seriously doubting that the feather would *tell* him *anything*.

"One, two, three!" The fan turned on and I could hear the feather say (isn't that weird?), "Yurnia," in the softest, gentlest voice I had ever heard. I was in Yurnia!

"Did you hear it?" the man asked. "I certainly did. You're in Yurnia. Go take your pass and leave." A pass on the table by the door had my name on it in blue and green, and the name "Yurnia" emblazoned on the front. I was so happy to leave!

Chapter Seven

"Good luck!" I whispered to Victoria, who was next in line. She gulped and disappeared into the dark room. I hoped and hoped she would be in the same dorm as I was.

I looked at my pass one more time. "That's odd, a completely new message," I said out loud, then felt stupid for talking to myself.

Welcome to Yurnia. Please keep this pass with you at all times. You will find Yurnia in the second chamber. Go through the door, and head up the staircase to the right. At the top will be a guard, whose name is Amber. She will need to see your pass; she will scan it and hand it back to you. Step inside the opening that appears. You will see two doors, one Girls,' one Boys.' Inside the "Girls" door, your bed is #8.

I followed the directions and soon found myself in front of the guard. I was sort of nervous, but this seemed to be one of the easier things at Dream Ring, so I pretended to be cool and collected.

Amber was tall, with straight, blond hair that reached her lower back. She looked more like a human than Cowcatine, but still a little strange. I'm sure I'll get to know her better if I see her every time I enter this dorm!

"Hi," I said.

"Hello," she said in a deep, deep voice. "Welcome, first-year Yurnian."

"Um, yeah, I guess," I answered.

"I need to see your pass."

I handed it to her.

She looked at it for a moment and then said, "See you, Ava."

"Bye." I walked through the opening that appeared and walked into the room marked "Girls." My bed was the one by the window.

"Yes!"

"What are you doing up here so early?" A loud voice made me whirl around. A girl with wild red hair and an ugly wart on her nose stood right behind me. She held a big blue duffel bag in her arms.

"I ate fast, and then I was first in line for the sorting," I said. "Are you in Yurnia too?"

"Well, of course I am," she replied snottily. "Why else would I be here? Teams aren't allowed to go into each others' rooms."

"I didn't know," I said under my breath. "Don't blame *me*."

"So, what's your name?" the girl asked in her snotty, loud voice. "I'm Ella."

"I'm Ava," I said. "Where are you from?"

"A small town in New Hampshire; you probably haven't heard of it," Ella said absentmindedly.

"I'm from New Hampshire, too!" I exclaimed.

"What town?" she asked in a slightly nicer tone. She grinned, revealing straight white teeth.

"Evansville," I said.

"That's where *I* live!" she said. "What school did you go to?"

"Evansville Middle," I answered.

"Me, too! How strange, that we haven't even noticed each other in the halls.

"Well, it's nice that we have something in common, but I'd better start unpacking," she said.

"What bed number?" I wondered out loud.

"I think the pass said Number Nine, but I'll have to check," she said and pursed her lips.

Life isn't fair. First I had to be some freak witch girl, and then I had to be the freak witch girl who has to sleep next to an even freakier witch girl.

"Yes! Number Nine!" she shouted. "That's my lucky number!"

How she was able to sneak up here so fast, I had no clue, because I had thought I was the first one to get sorted. But she was definitely a first-year. I knew snotty girls like her. The whole act was because they felt scared, with no friends around. Part of me felt bad because Ella probably didn't have any witch friends. She would probably stop being such a brat once she made a few friends here in Neptune.

Suddenly, a whole group of girls walked in, chattering happily. Victoria spotted me and came over to my bed.

"So what bed do you have?" I asked, crossing my fingers that she would be close to me.

"Hmm, I think the pass said Number Seven," she said. "What number is this one?"

"Number Eight!" I said excitedly. "We'll be right across from each other!"

"Awesome!" she said. "Let's start unpacking." We grabbed our duffel bags and started refolding our clothes and putting them into the little dressers by our bed.

After I arranged my clothes, I dug into a small pocket of my duffel bag. My toothbrush, brush, floss, and other personal products were in a little bag in there. I hung the bag on the knob of my dresser drawer.

A few minutes later I had finished unpacking, and, boy, was I tired! I changed into my pajamas, brushed my teeth in the communal bathroom the size of my bedroom at home (not really, but it was huge: five sinks, five showers, and three stalls!) that we shared, and flopped into bed. My pillow seemed extra comfy tonight: I fell asleep in the first few minutes that my head was resting on the soft flannel.

"Pssst! Are you awake?"

"I am now," I groaned sleepily, putting my pillow over my head.

"I can't sleep," a voice said.

"Why not?" I asked, wishing that whoever was talking would go tell someone else.

"If you'll take that pillow off your head, I'll tell you," the girl said.

Never give a girl an option of getting up in the middle of the night or not. Chances are, she'll "keep the pillow on," as it was in my case. I wish I could have avoided feeling sorry for the girl if I went back to sleep, but I couldn't. I moved the pillow.

To my surprise, the girl with the red hair—Ella—was sitting on my bed. She was a first-year like me, so she was probably scared to go to sleep on Neptune. I didn't blame her; I probably would've been the same way if I wasn't so tired. Either way, though, I'm never in a good mood when somebody wakes me up.

"Tell me, or I'm going back to sleep," I said.

"Well, the girls were telling scary stories tonight, and since this is Neptune, I thought, 'Maybe these things could happen.' And now I can't sleep."

"What time is it?" I asked.

"11:00 P.M.!" Ella said. *Oh, no. I probably made a fool out of myself by going to bed at, like, nine or something.*

"Nothing's here," I said. "Go to bed."

"I can't," Ella whined.

"Then go find someone who wants to stay up with you. I didn't get good sleep on the flight here, so now I'm going to catch up," I said.

Ella walked away when she realized she wasn't getting any sympathy. The room was dark, but I heard her rustling back into bed and snuggling into her covers, trying to fall asleep. Finally!

Chapter Eight

"It's morning already?" I grumbled, throwing the covers off me. A pillow hit me on the head.

"Yep! It's morning all right!" Vic hit me with another pillow.

I held my hands up. "I surrender!" I shouted. I grabbed my bag, went into the bathroom, and began brushing my hair.

Victoria ran in after me. "Today's the first day of classes!"

"Seriously?" I was *not* ready for this.

"Yeah, they announced it after you went to bed. Did you know that you went to bed at nine?"

"Yikes." So I *did* make a fool of myself! "What time did *you* go to bed?" I crossed my fingers, hoping to hear an early time, too.

"About 9:30. The others faded out around 10:45, but I didn't want you to be the only one in bed early, so I went to sleep, too."

I blew out a sigh of relief as I brushed my hair. Victoria was such a good friend!

While she brushed her teeth, I went back into our room to get the uniform that had been delivered last night.

They were very ugly clothes. I stepped into a stall to change.

All of my friends say I have a way with clothes. If my great-aunt Karen gives me an ugly white blouse, I turn it into a cute white top by cutting off the puffed sleeves, adding a few decorations or cool buttons, then writing on the back, "Don't be jealous." And if Uncle Henry gives me a pair of overalls, I'll wear them to school with a cute shirt underneath and my hair in braids.

When I came out of the stall, all the girls stopped to stare. Toothpaste dripped out of Victoria's mouth, and Ella actually dropped her brush.

"What?" I asked, knowing exactly what they were gaping at. I had cut my stuffy white blouse into a stylish white top by cutting most of the sleeves off and making it a lot less stuffy (which I was sure wasn't allowed). I wore a gold necklace that Great-Grandma Jane had given to me, gold hoop earrings adorned my ears, and I had put my hair in braids. I left the baggy maroon pants alone, but accessorized it all with dainty white flip-flops on my feet. We had to wear black robes over that, but I didn't mess those up; it would attract too much attention. But I didn't fasten the little buttons on the robe, so it wasn't really like my outfit was hidden.

"Your outfit, where'd you get it?" a girl named Miranda asked.

"Oh, this is the same outfit all of us were given; I just fixed it up a little." I looked in the mirror. "Does it look all right?" I asked, knowing the answer and their exact opinion of my new outfit.

"Yeah! Will you do it to mine?" Miranda asked.

"Sure." I took Miranda's outfit and cut it into a less formal top and handed it back to her. Soon a line formed for me to turn everyone's blouse into a stylish top, although they weren't all the same. I like to say that the 'creative juices' flowed differently in each blouse.

"Yurnia's going to be stylin'!" Victoria said as she put on her top and silver earrings to match. "We're leaving Talania in the dust!"

When we were all ready, the girls of Yurnia filed out the door to breakfast, me hoping I wouldn't get detention for my uniform and also hoping that maybe we wouldn't have to wear a uniform for the *entire* year. And hopefully most girls chose to button their robes, so it wouldn't be quite as obvious!

We ate breakfast the same way we ate dinner. I wished for two mini-bagels with strawberry cream cheese and a glass of milk. It was delicious!

After we had eaten our fill, Licklici stood up to get our attention. She looked even more beautiful today, in a long purple dress with white robes and small white slippers. Big, sparkling diamonds hung from her ears. She kind of looked like what I had always imagined a goddess to look like.

"Today is our first day of classes," Licklici said in her beautiful voice. "Under your plate, you will find two pieces of paper and a pencil. Please fill out the form and wish for another copy."

I looked at the form. This is what it looked like after I had filled it out:

ATTENTION, FIRST-YEARS!

Mandatory Classes:

   Flying (only for first-years)
   Powers against Evil Witchcraft
   Musical Magic against Evil

Draw a symbol on at least 3 classes, indicating you will be taking the class.

   Medication Using Magic __
   Star-Gazing ☺
   Fortune Telling ☺
   Woodworking to Create Magical Creatures __
   Wishful Thinking ☺
   Technology with Magic __

The second page looked like this:

Now fill out your name, bed #, date, and house:

   Name: Ava
   Bed Number: #8
   Date: August 14
   House: Yurnia

I wished for another copy, and it appeared. This wishing stuff could really come in handy sometimes. If only it worked outside of the main hall!

"Now, please send your original copy away and wish for a schedule," Licklici said. I did so, and a schedule now sat in front of me. I looked it over carefully, memorizing it in case it got lost. "Go get the books you received in your dorms this morning from the Dream Ring Staff for this year because classes start in fifteen minutes."

Victoria and I hopped up and ran out of the big hall to our dorm. Amber carefully looked over our passes and nodded. We sprinted through the hole in the wall and ran to get our books, trying not to be late on the first day.

⚘

"What's your first class?" Victoria asked as we sprinted down the halls, not knowing where to find the classroom.

"Uh, Stargazing, I think," I said, looking at my schedule. Oh my. Stargazing is probably the most boring of all the choices on Earth! And then I thought with ill humor, *and Neptune.*

While our teacher told us about herself (boring!), I zoned out and totally daydreamed for the whole class. I don't even remember the teacher's name. And Victoria was sitting across from me making things to decorate the wall space above her bed, only half-listening.

"So what was her name?" I asked as we walked down the hall to the next class.

"Professor Eleema, I think," Victoria replied.

"That's an interesting name," I said casually as we walked down the hall. "Is she nice?"

"Nice enough to give you an A, or whatever they give you here if you look like you're listening."

I listened very carefully in my next class, Powers Against Evil Witchcraft. My teacher was Professor Gophersmocker. He is married, his wife teaches Flying, his favorite color is black, and he is the head football coach. I guess today is the day to just meet your teachers, because I certainly didn't learn anything school-ish or magical.

Dinner was at 7:00 tonight. I went down to the main hall, and a *bird* was waiting ON my dinner plate! Eww! But it held a letter addressed to me, so I took the envelope from it and wished for a dead mouse to appear on the floor, hoping that maybe that bird actually *liked* dead mice. The bird took it and flew away. I opened the letter after wishing for a clean plate, which promptly appeared and took the place of the dirty one.

Dear Ava,

How are you adjusting on Neptune? I want you to be aware of a terrible thing on Neptune right now. The evil sorcerer, Widdidorm, has recently been spotted—he had been missing for over twenty-five years—so he is out for revenge. He went to school at Dream Ring. You cannot trust a man named Mr. Minaga, who might be on Neptune somewhere. He is known to have been friends with Widdidorm. If he gets you by yourself, scream and point your wand at him and shout, "Blind!" He will be momentarily blinded and fall to the floor. You take that time to run. I hope I haven't scared you too much—Dream Ring is supposed to be a fun and educational experience. I will be coming up at the end of first semester to see how you are doing. If you need me earlier, I will come. Watch out for Mr. Minaga and you will be good to go.

Love, Mom

P.S. Have you mastered the food-wishing thing? I did it a lot quicker than the rest of my friends. Haha!

Strange. I did, too.

Then I thought—*my first letter from Mom while I'm on a new planet, and it includes a death warning! Plus, my only self-defense is a wand—that I don't own yet. Where do I get one of those? Mom, why did you leave so many holes in this letter!?*

Tonight I stayed up later with all the girls in my room. They talked about stuff like boys and clothes. Definitely girly stuff, and boring, too. Victoria was pretending to like it, so I did, too. Later, when everyone else went to bed, she and I talked about stuff we liked, for example, sports, teachers, families, and embarrassing moments. The last topic is usually the most girly we get. I mean, sure, we talk about boys, too, but not obsessively, like some of the other girls in Yurnia.

Today I woke up wishing and hoping that what I dreamed about last night would not happen to me. I was in a dark room, the corner to be exact, and the door was locked. Someone in a cape was coming towards me, and I didn't like the look on his face. The only thing I can't remember about this dream is the face. I wish I remembered so I could seriously avoid this person.

Today was our first real day in classes, and it was interesting.

Chapter Nine

"I am Mrs. Gophersmocker. On most occasions, I would have you call me 'Professor Gophersmocker' but, since that is my husband's title, I will be Missus to you. You are here to learn flying. How many of you here were comfortable flying up here on your broom?"

About two-thirds of us raised our hands. Victoria and I did.

"Okay, good! But I'll let you in on a little secret."

This situation was weird. This *place* was weird, but we've already covered that topic.

We were standing in a field, our brooms in our hands. It was kind of strange—there were mattresses spread out all over the field—probably emergency landing stations for us first-years.

"The secret is,"—she paused for dramatic effect—"that you were *not* the ones flying your brooms. The professors were helping you fly. You first-years have no idea yet how to fly a broom! But now is the time to learn."

I was disappointed. How could the professors at Dream Ring do that to us? I had really felt like I knew how to fly, and the feeling had been wonderful.

"Okay. Now that that's over with, we'll start our class. Place your broom carefully on the ground. Now place your hand over it at about your hip's height, that's a good child, and say calmly, 'Hover.' The broom should come to you."

I followed her directions and my broom snapped into my hand. Cool!

Somehow I had the idea that the broom was not held above the ground by my power. It was really *hovering*.

"Now. Face forwards, away from the bristles of the broom. Slide onto the broomstick, but don't straddle the broom. Ella, you have to sit on the broom*stick*, not the end that you sweep with. You'll get used to the discomfort. This is like your car; it's liberating—now enjoy it." I shifted onto the broomstick. It was uncomfortable, but it was liberating. I could go anywhere with this broom. I could fly. This was definitely the coolest part of being… I hated to say it… a witch.

"We'll start flying now, but we will only fly a couple of feet above the ground. We made the mistake last year of flying at about forty feet… and we'll just say it didn't end well."

I gulped. What if I fell off? That would be so embarrassing!

"Now, when you flew here to Neptune, you directed your broom by pressing buttons or using hand gestures. Here you will use voice commands to direct your broom. To go, you will say 'Oomba'; to stop, you will say 'Tarum.'"

I giggled. "Oomba Tarum." My broom started to go and then stopped abruptly. I giggled again.

"Miss Ava Popolis. Wait until you are given directions to start." Her eyes grew very wide. "And *what* are you *wearing*?"

One of the boys mumbled a comment about my outfit. I pretended not to hear and said, "Well, Mrs. Gophersmocker, I felt the need to give my uniform a makeover." I knew it was sorta disrespectful, but the truth hurts sometimes.

She ignored me, and kept the class going. Thank goodness I didn't get a detention!

"Now, everyone, keep your broomsticks level and say 'Oomba.' If you feel you're going too fast, you say 'Wols.' Your broom will fly in a straight line. If you're going to bump into something, just stop your broom, okay? Go."

There was a chorus of 'Oombas,' and slowly our brooms took off. I wished that Mrs. Gophersmocker had told us how to go faster, but I figured she had done that purposely.

After we had flown for a few minutes, Mrs. Gophersmocker had us slow down and stop. "Now, dismount," she ordered, like we were on some sort of horse. "And then pick up your broom. If it tries to shoot into the air, well, don't let it."

"How?" Ella asked.

"Um, stop it, then SLOWLY"—she emphasized this word to the entire class—"aim it at the ground."

We all followed her directions, except a boy named Henry. When he tried to pick up his broom, it shot into the air, dragging him with it. He snickered and hopped onto his broom mid-air. Then he flew in a straight line for a couple of minutes (much to Mrs. Gophersmocker's disapproval at him being so high up) and then aimed his broom back at the ground. He quickly said 'Wols' as his broom picked up speed, and it obeyed him. He smoothly dismounted, receiving a high-five from the kid named Josh. Those two were going to be trouble-makers, I could definitely tell.

Chapter Ten

When I got out my pass to show to my next teacher for Fortune Telling, it had a new message on it:

"Go to the main hall to receive your messengers."

I could barely read it; the font was so small, but I could read 'main hall.' So I picked up my backpack and headed there, carrying my broom with me.

It was a long walk to the main hall, and I suddenly had a good idea. Why not try out my broom, since I'm outside and I kinda know how to control it?

"Hover." My broom snapped into my hand, and I hopped on and quickly instructed it to 'Oomba.' It took off at a brisk pace, which was okay, since I was going to be late if I didn't hurry.

The only problem with this (genius) idea was that I didn't know how to steer. So several times I had to say 'Tarum' and hop off. Then I would manually redirect my broom and hop back on.

When I was about twenty feet away from the main hall, I hopped off my broom and carried it the rest of the way. I figured there was no point in getting in trouble the second day.

Well, it turns out that a couple of other students had had the same idea as me and the teachers found out. We were all assigned after-school detentions before we entered the main hall. Detention at Dream Ring? *Pathetic.* This school was supposed to be fun!

Once we were all in the main hall, Licklici came into the room. She was dressed in maroon robes, and she had on elegant diamond earrings with a matching necklace. I think she was barefoot, but you couldn't tell because her robes covered her feet.

"Welcome, students," she said in her pretty voice, which was magically, like, twenty times louder than most voices. "Today you will get your messengers."

We started to chatter excitedly in anticipation. "Quiet, students," Licklici said. "I'm not finished. Your messengers will be your letter carriers while you're on Neptune. They can fly anywhere on Neptune to deliver messages. They can also fly to Earth, but can deliver only to witches and wizards there. You do NOT pick your birds; they pick you. There are no exchanges. Your messengers will not die. Your bird's gender is your gender. You are required to name your birds.

"Do not panic as we unlock the cages. These are new birds, about six months old, and they're not totally trained. They will most likely fly around at the ceiling for twenty seconds or so, and then they will land at their student. If you panic or make a lot of noise, they will be frightened, so please be silent. Thank you. Ready?" We nodded.

"One more thing. The bird that you will receive is your State Bird, or your Nation's Bird in other cases. So you might want to do some research about your bird. Witches and wizards can only have birds for messengers; that is an ancient rule. Here we go!"

She gave a command in a strange language, and suddenly about two hundred birds entered the main hall. It was hard not to panic, but I stayed silent. Victoria started to shake next to me because she was so scared. See, I'm an animal lover, always have been, but Victoria has been afraid of animals for most of her existence. This all stems from the ancient, beloved dog of Mrs. Petty, her neighbor, who bit her when she was three. Oh, the trauma. She clenched my hand tightly. I sent her my best best-friend vibes telling her not to be afraid, that it was okay, and I think she relaxed a little.

Ella got pooped on. So did Josh. They sorta freaked out (Ella started shrieking and screaming), but I think the two of them were a little amused, too. I giggled silently.

A violet colored bird landed on the table right in front of me. The messenger pecked my arm and then hopped into my lap. I laughed and gently petted its purple feathers. Then it pecked me again, so I looked at its foot. On it was a message tied with a red string. I unrolled it and read the message.

I want to be your messenger. Purple Finch.

I gave the messenger a gentle hug. "I want you to be my bird," I murmured. "I'm going to name you Violet."

The messenger was purple-colored with a pretty stripe down its back, and it reminded me of home and my favorite flower on Earth. Violet nuzzled me, and I hugged it back. It was so cute! I couldn't wait to send my first letter!

(After doing some research, I discovered that its coloring was really more male, but Licklici had said that our messengers would be the same gender that we were, and I was female. Duh! Finally I decided that Violet was just special.)

Victoria's messenger was fawn-colored with a tinge of purple, and it had the calmest disposition I could ever imagine. It just sat in Victoria's lap and looked at her with its huge eyes. Victoria smiled bravely and petted it tentatively. I laughed and showed Victoria Violet.

"I think I'm going to name my messenger Fawn," Victoria said timidly. "She's so cute."

"I know. She's adorable," I agreed. "But I wonder why she's a different color than mine," I mused. "Maybe she's just different."

"Yeah," Victoria agreed. "I still love her."

"Totally."

I looked at my pass. It said "Free Period, 45 minutes."

"Let's go back to our rooms and write our first letter with them!" I said. "You know, since we have a free period."

Victoria grinned.

Licklici said, "Okay, students. You now have a free period. Please head back to your dorms. You MAY fly, but if you go more than twenty feet in the air, you have a double detention.

And your messengers will be taken away. Please do not fly too fast. I'm trusting you."

We cheered. TWENTY FEET? I hadn't dared over FIVE feet yet. This was going to be a blast.

We all flew safely back to our dorms, where we proceeded to lounge and write our first letters with our new messengers. Nobody got a double detention, thankfully!

Dear Mom,

I am getting adjusted to Dream Ring. We just got our birds this afternoon and this is the first letter I will send with my messenger. Her name is Violet. She really likes bird food, berries, and insects, so please reward her for her travels.

I have made friends here, and Victoria's also adjusting. We had our first flying lesson today, and I love the feeling of being in the air on my broom. Today Licklici let us fly twenty feet in the air! I don't think she got the memo that Mrs. Gophersmocker told us not to fly very high at all, so we had fun breaking the rules. (Which it wasn't really, since we had permission to do so from the headmistress herself.)

I am being a pretty good girl ~ only have one detention, when I flew to class because I was going to be late. But don't worry; about thirty other students did it too, so we all have after-school detentions. We have to wash the teachers' brooms. Ewow, right?

I miss you and Dad a lot. I have to go. Victoria and Ella and Kathryn just found a vent that leads to the teachers' lounge and you can hear everything. Can't miss that opportunity!

Miss you.

Love, Ava

p.s. I am in Yurnia!

I sent my letter to Mom with Violet right away. I gave her a kiss on the head and opened the window for her. She flew out, my letter on her tiny clawed foot, tied with a blue ribbon. I hope that she would get it to Mom soon.

Dear Ava,

Thank you for writing! Violet is extremely adorable, much better than my messenger (but don't tell Bunny I said that)!

I hope that that is the LAST detention you receive this year. The parents will visit for parent-teacher conferences after first semester ends, and I don't want you to be on Licklici's bad side. If you are, it's not good!

Your friend Caleb has been e-mailing you constantly lately. I had to e-mail him and tell him that you were away. What else do you want me to say?

Your father and I miss you dearly every single day. Have a great time!

Love, Mom

p.s. I hope you know that Dad would write if he could.

p.p.s. I gave the very best of feed and insects to Violet! ☺

Dear Mom,

Thanks for your letter! I really miss you and Dad, but I'm having a pretty good time here. I'm super busy, though; I'll try to write as often as I can, but I don't know when I'll have the chance.

Love you!
Ava

Chapter Eleven

It's the beginning of September, and it's like full-blown winter here on Neptune. We've gotten through two weeks of school. *I* have gotten through it. Amen. I've begun to find a new normal after the whole "you're a witch" deal, and I've gotten fairly used to brooms and magic and taking classes on another planet.

Today we got news in the big hall. There's going to be a big storm on Neptune.

"Attention, students!" A voice filled the big hall. "Please head to your dorms. An ice storm is coming to Neptune. It will be in our presence for about three days. Food has been stored in your kitchen in the dorm. Please note that your messengers cannot work during this storm, so the latest that you can send messages is tonight at 10 P.M. Please warn your parents of the ice storm so that they do not send your messenger back until next Tuesday.

"Do not leave your dorms without permission. During this storm our magic will not work, so it will get extremely cold in your dorms. Please try to stay warm. Extra robes will be given to your dorm, one for every person. Please make a fire in your fireplace. I suggest that you keep your doors closed as much as possible so that the heat will stay in your rooms. Good luck. Now hurry!"

We all walked quickly to the big closet in the main hall, where we retrieved our brooms. I was scared. Just how cold would the weather be? I mean, it was *cold* in ice storms on Earth, but Neptune was the furthest planet from the sun. Would we survive?

I giggled at the thought of being *frozen in terror.*

We flew quickly to our dorms, at about seventy feet in the air, the wind making my breath quicken and my cheeks turn red with a joyful briskness. Today was the first time that I did the new trick that Mrs. Gophersmocker had taught us in flying class about four days ago. "EGGBOMB!" I screamed at the top of my lungs. I leaned in until I was practically lying on my broomstick, as we had to straddle the broom for this trick. A door opened on the roof without me having to do anything, and my broom flew through it at top speed. I was literally diving on a broom. I flew through the door and bounced onto my bed, unharmed. My broom lay next to me.

"WOO-HOO!" I screamed excitedly. It was so much fun! I mean, flying through a roof on a broomstick! I was elated.

Several of my classmates chose to Eggbomb, too. I wonder why it's called that…

We all kind of waited to get ready for the ice storm until it started. It sounds dumb, but that's just what we did. I think we knew we would all be in the same room for three days, so we figured we'd have plenty time to prepare.

Clunk. Bonk. Clunk. The sound startled me as I sat writing my letter to Mom. I ran over to the window and looked out. Chunks of ice—not rain—chunks—were falling from the sky at a quick pace. They plopped onto the roof with a plunk. I felt a little unnerved and unsure—none of us had ever experienced anything like it. I sent up a quick prayer and wrote my letter at a faster pace.

Dear Mom,

We're having a huge ice storm here on Neptune. It's supposed to last for three days! Our powers won't work during it, so it's going to be extremely cold. Please do NOT send Violet back until Tuesday, because she will be in great danger if she tries to fly through the storm. Please send Caleb this e-mail:

"Dear Caleb: Sry I have not been able 2 write lately. I am going 2 a school that is very strict, and we r not allowed to e-mail. I'll e-mail u when I can, but it won't be very often. I'm really sry. I miss being at *the beach. Haha! We had a lot of fun this summer!*

~Ava

p.s. Please say hi to your sister 4 me! ☺"

END

Say hi to Dad for me, 'kay? Miss u lots! Love, Ava

I handed the letter to Violet and sent her out. She flew bravely into the wind to go deliver my note before it was too late.

I sent my letter at 9:00, then I started preparing. The ice storm was predicted to *really* start at 11:00.

I straightened my bed and dresser, then put on my warmest clothes. When I was finished dressing, I was wearing tights, sweatpants, a tank top, shirt, sweater, jacket, and two pairs of socks. I kept my wavy, blond hair down as a sort of blanket for my back, and put on a hat. Two coats went on top of all of that.

Other girls were putting on just as many clothes as me. When we were nearly ready for the ice storm, I glanced at my watch: 9:59. I was starting to overheat in so much clothing.

My next thought was food. I headed into the kitchen, where about twelve other girls were lounging. Since there were about 45 girls in Yurnia, there was a pretty big kitchen. It had all of the appliances, plus one extra refrigerator. Licklici had prepared us well, with sandwich-makings, eggs, milk, dairy, and lots of cookies. She knew that we girls had cravings for desserts. There were also makings for cheesecake, gooey butter cake, dirt cake, and ice cream sundaes. Yummy.

I dished myself a bowl of ice cream and poured a good amount of chocolate syrup over it. Then I sprayed some whipped cream on top. Mmmm-Mmmm. I also put a spoonful of Oreo crumbs on top of all that: perfection.

I dug into my dessert while I watched TV with Victoria. In Yurnia we were allowed to have television, but with limited channels. We had TLC, Style, Nickelodeon, Disney, and News Channel "76 Neptune." While Randy helped another distressed woman find her perfect wedding dress on *Say Yes to the Dress,* I chowed down on my perfect food.

Suddenly Randy's face disappeared. The power had gone out! Thank goodness the refrigerator would never go out; Licklici had put an eternal charm on it that would keep it on for forever.

Victoria and I had some old-fashioned girl time then. We sat and talked about everything.

Victoria brought up the subject of Caleb, so I started filling her in on everything that's been going on with him.

"Who's Caleb?" Kathryn asked as she walked past. "Do you have a *boyfriend*?"

"No," I responded, feeling my ears turn red. "He's not my boyfriend."

"Then what is he?"

"Well, okay, you see, um, well…" I felt myself stuttering a little, and I knew it was because I was trying to hide what I felt about Caleb—"When I went on vacation this year we met some kids that were renting the condo next to us. We hung out with them every day on the beach. One boy's name was Caleb—he's my age. He has a sister that's seven, and a cousin that's also seven. I played with them a lot, and then Caleb and I would hang out. When we left we exchanged e-mail addresses, so we've been e-mailing a lot. It's been fun. He's kinda cute."

Kathryn slumped into a chair. "I don't have a boyfriend or anything."

"He's not my boyfriend," I pointed out again. "He's just a friend. Who happens to be a boy."

"Ohhhh-kay. Yeah, sure." She winked. I threw a pillow at her. Whoops, that sure was a mistake. The rest of the girls took what they thought was a hint and started a pillow fight.

In the middle of our pillow war, we heard a knock. We were bundled up like idiots when it wasn't even cold, and we were shrieking while we whacked pillows at each other. I'm sure we looked pretty immature to Licklici, who happened to be the one at the door.

We stopped in action when she opened the door. She was dressed in a thick white dress with white boots. She had on a snug white coat that looked pretty fashionable, too, and the hood formed a frame around her honey-blond hair. She carried a large bag.

"Hello, ladies," she said in her beautiful voice. "I see that you are..." She paused. I mean, what can you say to forty-five teenagers that were acting like morons?

"...having... fun," she finished.

We blushed and put our pillows down. One teenager asked bluntly, "Are we in trouble?"

"No," she said. "I came to help you prepare. What are you all *wearing*?"

"Warm clothes," the same girl said. "Don't we look hideous?"

"Yes, quite hideous," Licklici said. "I brought less...er... ridiculous clothes for you."

While she got her materials out of the bag, we cleaned up the pillows and made ourselves look presentable. When we came out of the big bedroom, a fire was roaring in the fireplace of the kitchen (Licklici had put a spell on it, so it would be magically working throughout the ice storm—*her* powers were still working) and the room was toasty.

Some of us made hot cocoa while the rest of us got into the outfits that Licklici had brought us.

Licklici had brought us a beautiful outfit that was both warm and stylish: a white flannel long-sleeved shirt that said 'Dream Ring' on it; maroon sweatpants (with maroon cotton tights underneath); and a maroon robe, along with white slippers and a white hat.

After we had all changed into our outfits, Licklici helped us by making firewood appear, and then she wished us luck. "I must go now. I still have to go to Talania's dorms to help them. Good luck!" And with that, she snapped her fingers and disappeared.

Chapter Twelve

The ice storm raged outside while we all huddled inside our warm robes. Licklici had said not to take the outfit off until the ice storm was over. I thought the idea of wearing the same clothes for three days was kind of disgusting, but I went along with it. I figured Licklici knew what she was talking about.

We played games and ate ice cream the first night. Then we went to bed, snuggling under the extra blankets Licklici had brought us. I woke up in the middle of the night and I couldn't stop shaking. The storm had released its full fury outside, and it was so cold. I was colder than I had been the time my family went camping in February and it had snowed. Colder than that.

Victoria was awake, too, just shaking silently. I tiptoed over to her bed and sat down next to her. Since they were full-sized beds, there was room for me, too. I brought all of my blankets, and we slept in her bed under twice the blankets, hip to hip. It was warmer, and it gave Victoria courage.

Sometimes Victoria is just so quiet and afraid that I feel bad for her. I looked at this as an adventure, but I'm pretty sure she didn't. Her tears proved my theory correct.

"Victoria, it's okay," I consoled her. "We'll be all right."

"I know," she whimpered. "I'm just so cold." Her teeth were chattering uncontrollably, as were mine.

I realized then that if we all slept under just the three quilts that we each had, we were in danger of freezing. So I woke everybody up.

"Okay, everybody!" I shouted. "It's too cold to be in our own beds without having our blood stirred. So, everybody give me thirty jumping-jacks!" A good half of the girls ignored me and went back to sleep. This was worse than I thought. "C'mon!" I shouted. "Thirty!"

Finally everybody did thirty jumping jacks. Then best friends crawled into each other's beds, and we all slept with a partner and twice the blankets. It was too cold *not* to.

At last that horrible night was over, and we all woke up shivering. I was so cold, it wasn't even funny. At least half of the Yurnia girls started crying, me included. This was *not* fun. I resolved to send a letter to Mom when it was all over telling her that I was coming home.

That day all we did was lie on the comfortable furniture. Every thirty minutes we all got up and did thirty jumping jacks.

But that night we were ready. We put our mattresses on the floor next to heating vents (not that it would do much good) and all slept next to each other. It was a little warmer, but we were still miserable.

The second day of the storm, we were all a little used to the cold. Besides, we had a happy thought: After today, there was only one more day of this! Even though it was just raining now, it was still dark, cold, and depressing.

One of our laptop computers had a work-charm on it—so its battery never died and it never quit working—and we used that to e-mail boys and girls from the other dorms to check in on them. From Yurnia boys, Josh Wilson was our main e-mailer. He was making his guys do the same as we were, trying to get their blood moving with jumping jacks and push-ups.

><~~><

The second day was actually fun. I got everybody to play a new game that we made up. Broom tag! (Our living room was quite large, so we could all play at once!) Although our magic and powers weren't working, our brooms were always functioning, no matter what, so we played it for an hour in the living room without realizing that we were truly cold. A little hot cocoa helped. Then we played other games on our brooms, which kept our minds off the fact that we were numb in places (I couldn't feel my hands or feet, and my legs were going soon; I could hardly walk).

At the beginning of the storm, we split into nine groups. One group would make breakfast, another lunch, another dinner. There were nine because there were nine meals that we would have during the ice storm. My group was called "The Purple Flying Monkeys."

The Monkeys were in charge of dinner tonight. I made dirt cake, Victoria made cheesecake, and Kathryn made a gigantic smoothie with the help of two other girls, named Tanya and Gabriella. We had a fruity dessert dinner. It was fun and it got everybody's spirits up because it was so sugary and good.

✺

The third and last day was the worst, 'cause we were all *so* ready for the ice storm to be over. This had been the worst experience of my life. Ah, it had had its perks; I mean, we had all been left alone for three days and we had broken the rules (no brooms in the house; for dinner you have to have a basic meal). But on the third day, we basically forgot that. We were so sick of the ice storm that we pretty much just ate, cried, and slept all day. We barely did any jumping jacks. I was numb everywhere. The bathroom... well, let me just say that you only went there a few times a day because it was so cold.

On the fourth day, when I woke up, my ears hurt. I was shivering, but I could move my arms and legs. Then I realized that my ears hurt because of the silence! There was no more angry storm pounding on the roof! It was over! IT WAS OVER! I was so excited that I woke everyone up and we celebrated together. We rode our brooms and danced to celebrate our working limbs. We ate food again because we were actually hungry for the first time in two days. We were alive! We had made it! And the sun was SHINING! I mean, as much as the sun can shine in Neptune. It *is* eight planets away from the sun.

I changed my clothes and went to the bathroom without shaking. I was able to SHOWER! I was so excited. There was *hot water!* And Violet would come back! There are not enough exclamation points in the world to describe my elation!

The ice storm was over! YES! We had survived it!!!

Chapter Thirteen

We hadn't been outside in three days, so Licklici and Mrs. Gophersmocker took the whole freshman class on a broom ride. We were pretty well-behaved, but we were really hyper. The day was only slightly chillier than the other days on Neptune, and we could wear jeans and T-shirts, and of course a sweatshirt or a coat. Just that thought made us giddy. We could sleep on top of the sheets tonight because the heat was back on inside! Oh, what a good feeling.

We did everything outside now. For the whole next week we ate outside, we played outside, all of our classes were outside. We all just soaked up sunshine. I think the teachers were okay with that, because they were sick of their dorms, too. (That vent is very helpful! Eavesdropping on the teachers' lounge can be pretty handy sometimes.)

Violet returned with a letter from Mom.

Dear Ava,

How was the ice storm? I sincerely hope that you are okay. The 'mysterious storm' on Neptune was all over the Internet here on Earth, but nobody suspects anything. They all just think it's interesting.

Violet was very sweet. She stayed in my closet the whole time because I didn't want your father to see her. She really loves me because I feed her a lot of nuts and berries.

Do you know how cold the weather got during the ice storm? I'd be interested to know.

I miss you dearly. Your father sends his love also. I can't wait to see you. Only one more month!

Love, Mom

Mom was sweet. I missed her too. Only one more month 'til first semester's over!? Hmmm... this semester had gone by quickly! I quickly wrote and sent a letter away with Violet.

For a long time after the storm, the weather was colder on Neptune than it had been in August. But that didn't stop us from being outside as much as possible!

Chapter Fourteen

I had my first class of Musical Magic Against Evil one week after the ice storm. As I walked into class, I began to feel tired. I had been perfectly awake the moment before, but now I just wanted to sleep. What was up with me? I shook myself hard. I had heard that this class was not easy, and I wanted to get a good grade in it.

"Hello, everyone. I am Mr. Minaga. I will be your professor for Musical Magic Against Evil for the rest of the year. My hobbies are sleeping,"—did he just look at me?—I yawned—"eating dessert, and playing volleyball with my wife. I have two kids, both teenagers. They are very much like me. I hope that this class is not too hard, but it will have some challenges." I swear when he said "My hobbies are sleeping" he looked straight at me with a menacing stare and raised his eyebrows a tiny bit. What did that mean?

Mr. Minaga was about six feet tall, and he had brown hair buzzed close to his scalp. His eyes were a very sharp, crystal-clear blue, and he was clean-shaven. He wore black robes, scuffed-up business shoes, and a black crystal watch ticking loudly on his wrist. His movements were slick and sure, but something about him seemed a little crazy. He looked like there was something inside of him that was driving him a little off-kilter. Very odd.

But this professor was funny. I could tell I was going to like this class. All the more reason to be awake for it. But I felt *so* tired. I just wanted a pillow. That's it—just one pillow.

Then it hit me.

Minaga. Minaga. I had heard that name somewhere before. *Minaga.* Where had I heard that name? Was it a magazine? No. Why would it be a magazine? I was on *Neptune.*

I felt my eyes start to close. Before I dropped off, I finally remembered where I had heard that name. He was the guy Mom had mentioned in her letter. He was the one who was supposed to be friends with Widdidorm! Oh, no. This was seriously bad. What should I do? I was almost asleep now.

As I fought my droopy eyelids, an idea came to me that would solve my problem for about ten minutes. "Um, Mr. Minaga?" I asked politely, raising my hand. I knew that this could be potentially embarrassing, but I had to get away from the creeper.

"Yes, Miss Ava?" How he knew my name, I had no idea.

"I have to go to the bathroom. May I be excused?" I gave him a look that was pretty spectacular considering that I have only been a teenager for about two months. My smile seemed sweet and innocent, I thought.

"You may be excused, Ava. Hurry back."

"Thank you." I grabbed my purse and ran out the door. I knew I had to get out of there.

Once out of the room, I slumped in the corridor. I still fought the urge to fall asleep, so I moved farther down the hall. There I felt more awake, and my head felt clearer.

I congratulated myself on not falling asleep while I was that close to some kind of a supportive evil person. I had already met the evil sorcerer Widdidorm, and another meeting did not sound pleasant. He was not my buddy, or anything close to it.

I put my head in my hands and thought for a few minutes. What was I going to do? The rest of my classmates were still in there. I had to get them out. Or something. Were we all in danger? *Think. Think. Concentrate. What would Mom say or do?* I thought. Well, in her letter, she had said that if I met him to say "Blind!" and then run away, quickly. But she had also said to only do that if I met him alone, and I don't have a wand yet. I guess she didn't know he was one of my teachers. And what if the spell didn't work? What if I blinded one of my classmates, and that only made him mad? We hadn't learned a lot of magic yet, only basic stuff.

This was bad.

I returned to class without a plan. I vowed to stay awake, though, and not meet Widdidorm again.

When I returned to class, we were working on reading witch music. It consisted of a lot of gibberish put to a tune. "Craw shay de doo-dop pa-PAY! Pa-PAY! Craw shay de doo-dop pa-PAY! Maw-dops 'n' skeetos!" I think that the song meant, "I hope you enjoy our song. Our song! I hope you enjoy our song, ladies and gentlemen!" It didn't really make any sense, but then again, gibberish was pretty *out there*, too.

Finally, class was over. I hurried to the broom closet and grabbed my broom. I hopped on, and flew to my dorm. We had a 45-minute free period, and I *had* to send a letter to Mom.

Dear Mom,

Big uh-oh! Mr. Minaga, well, he's our Musical Magic Against Evil teacher! Today he was funny and charming, but I get the feeling that won't be the case the whole year. He almost put me to sleep, so I asked to go to the restroom. I felt better once I was outside the classroom. I just went along with the class the rest of the time. I don't know what to do! Please RE-PLY SOON! I really need help. My next class with him is Friday. And today is Monday. - ☹ - So I need, like, a lightning-fast reply, please! Give my love to Dad!

Help!

Ava

That night the only person that I talked to about Mr. Minaga was Victoria. She was a little scared, but she was also half-asleep when I told her. The next morning at breakfast, though, she realized the full effect of what I had said.

"You mean that Widdidorm might be communicating through Minaga?" she asked, incredulous. "He seemed like an okay guy."

"No, he is *not* okay. *Please* don't like him. I don't want you turning evil." I said it like a joke, but I wasn't really being funny. She laughed.

"You might wanna send a letter to your mom," Vic advised.

"Yeah. Hey, do we have flying today?" I asked.

"Yeah, at 11:00," Victoria replied. She tapped her wrist, like she was checking an imaginary watch, and grinned."Uh, that's in, like, a half-hour. Sorry, I gotta run. I still have to shower, and you know how long that takes me. Will you do my dishes please?" she asked.

"Sure."

"Thanks. You're a lifesaver!" And with that, she was off.

Since today wasn't a special day, we ate in the dorm kitchen instead of the big hall. Sadly, that meant we had to cook our own food and do our own dishes. Ever since the ice storm, we'd kept the arrangement of each group cooking one meal per day, and that's still how we operate. If your group cooks, your group does the dishes. It's been a pretty sweet system. Well, only if you're not on the team that cooks that day. You basically only have to cook one meal every three days, which isn't that bad.

For flying class, we were assigned partners; we were told that we were allowed to fly all over Neptune as long as we could see Dream Ring and we didn't go over one hundred feet in the air. Mrs. Gophersmocker was pretty cool in flying class. This was the third time we were given this assignment. It was to be an hour-long ride.

My partner was Josh Wilson. He's funny, but I don't *like* him or anything.

Josh and I rocketed to about seventy-five feet, then flew side-by-side for a couple of minutes. I looked beneath me and gasped at the beautiful landscape.

I could see what looked like a chain of mountains with hills and valleys a long way off. The sun was shining as much as it can on Neptune, and the light bounced off the beautiful, radiant colors. I saw all the colors of the rainbow, I think: blues, greens, oranges, reds, and yellows. And maybe some purples or indigos, too. I had never seen anything so gorgeous.

Then Josh suggested that we race, so we raced for, like, five minutes. In the end, he won, but that was only because my broom started to go out of control, and I had to slow down to keep from falling off.

We talked for a while about school. I sorta gave him hints about who Mr. Minaga was, and he was shocked when he finally figured it out. By that time, we needed to head back to Dream Ring's campus. We raced back, and then Eggbombed onto the special rug that Mrs. Gophersmocker had laid out for that purpose. As usual, it didn't hurt to collapse onto the thin fabric when you rocketed in headfirst from about fifty feet. If you Eggbomb correctly, you don't get hurt. If you don't do it correctly, you get a small headache. It was pretty awesome, considering the fact that you would dismount with almost guaranteed class.

The lesson ended with a lecture by Mrs. Gophersmocker on the proper way to do an Eggbomb. Then we were dismissed. I headed to Fortune Telling by way of broom, Eggbombing onto the carpet outside the classroom. It didn't even hurt.

Chapter Fifteen

Early one morning, I felt cold in bed for some reason. I was inside, where the temperature always adjusts to just how you and the others like it. But it just felt cold, you know, like the rest of the weather on Neptune. Like someone had forgotten to turn the heat on, and on Neptune, that's a serious crime. The heat is on year-round on our remote planet.

I opened my eyes and peeked out from under the covers. The room was pitch black, and it felt like the temperature was stationed somewhere below thirty degrees, which is very cold if you've ever been in the dorm room in Yurnia, Neptune. Actually, it's very cold *anywhere*.

I pulled on my maroon robe and a pair of slippers, and even slipped on my white hat from the ice storm. I glided out the Eggbomb hole on my broom while everyone was asleep. I needed some fresh air; never mind that it's 3 A.M., right?

I flew around for a while. A light mist was falling, but it didn't bother me because I was well-bundled against the cold. The air felt fresh and wonderful, and my spirit soared. It was fun out here, just me and my broom. Wouldn't it be magnificent to come out here every night?

There was just something about the air in Neptune. I couldn't put my finger on it, but I had a pretty good idea that it involved the fact that there was no pollution on Neptune, unlike Earth. How sad that regular humans couldn't breathe this air. We would all be so much healthier.

When I returned from my midnight ride—whoops, more like a three A.M. ride—Violet was waiting on the windowsill with a letter. I thanked her with a dead mouse and took the letter. She flew off to the cage where she lived when she wasn't delivering messages for me.

I read the letter right then and there. I mean, I might as well. It's not like I could fall asleep with the temperature inside the dorm…

Dear Ava,

Okay. The news about Mr. Minaga is not good. The second letter that you're receiving from Violet is for Licklici. I am requesting that you be excused from Musical Magic Against Evil. I explained that I do not approve of Mr. Minaga and that I do not think he is appropriate. If she is in a good mood, she will understand and excuse you from class. If she is not in a good mood, the answer will be a definite 'No,' and she will send me a letter explaining her decision. If she does say no, I will tell her about my feelings about Mr. Minaga at the parent-teacher conferences in two weeks.

I hope that you are being good and having fun. I can't wait to see you. Only two more weeks! Wow, time must feel like it's gone by fast for you. It always did to me when I was on Neptune. After the first semester, your powers will start to come in. I can't wait to see you! I know I already said that, but I'm very excited about my visit to Neptune. It's been years since I've been there. I crave some of that clean, fresh air.

Love, Mom ☺

I couldn't wait for Mom's visit. I just hoped that the teachers gave her good reports, because I knew that if they didn't, I was in *big* trouble.

And my powers would come in after first semester? Hmmm... that would be kinda weird. I mean, the thought of powers is sort of freaky if you dwell on it. I wondered what powers I would get.

I tried to sleep, but the cold kept me awake. It was *so* cold in the dorm. And none of the lights would turn on. Even the refrigerator wasn't on, which sort of freaked me out. The refrigerator *never* turned off. What did that mean?

Finally it was morning. I woke Victoria the minute it turned 9:00. She was shivering and pale. "I'm so co-co-cold," she chattered, her teeth clacking together. "And hungry." I laughed. Who could think of food when she was so cold? Only Victoria. She had always had a soft spot for cookies, but you couldn't tell by looking at her. She was a healthy weight.

I fixed her a peanut butter and jelly sandwich—the only thing that was, like, substantial food in our pantry, since the refrigerator was out. She ate it thankfully while we lounged on the couch, waiting for our friends to wake up. We didn't have classes today until noon, so most of the girls slept in. While we waited, we might have had a couple of cookies, too…

✎❀✎

A voice boomed overhead on the invisible speaker. "Attention, students! This is just a temporary power outage! I know that your refrigerators and appliances are out. The source of this temporary power outage is not the weather this time, but rather the evil sorcerer Widdidorm. He seems to wield more magic when the power is out—please stay calm. Hopefully, this will be over soon. Stay warm. It is sunny outside, so take a broom ride or something. The weather's not bad today."

We headed outside. Classes were canceled, so we could do whatever we wanted. The nerds were holding a study group for our upcoming math quiz (yes, we have math on Neptune), the popular kids were complimenting each other's wardrobe choices since today was out-of-uniform, and Mrs. Gophersmocker decided to supervise a broom ride that went around the entire planet of Neptune. I chose the broom ride. It would take all day, so I wouldn't have to be in the dreadfully cold dorm at all.

The ride was actually really cool. One kid almost fell off his broom, which was hilarious (and extremely dangerous), but other than that, there were no troubles. Neptune is beautiful, its green and blue clouds swirling around, and the atmosphere a hazy border. When Mrs. Gophersmocker wasn't looking, I slid down one of the rings. It literally made my heart soar. They were shockingly slippery, and I had to be really careful not to fall off. I slid for a couple of minutes while Mrs. Gophersmocker was explaining to a bunch of earnest listeners about the witch and wizard history of Neptune. She didn't even notice I was gone.

The rings were made up of various sizes and rocks of all different colors and textures, and they were deliciously cool to the touch—and *very icy*. I suppose that it would freeze your bottom if you stayed on one too long. Wouldn't that be sort of a hilarious predicament? I mean, imagine calling your mom. "Uh, hi, Mom. I'm frozen to Neptune's rings. I can't get unstuck." "I'll be there in a minute, honey!" I giggled at the thought.

While Mrs. Gophersmocker did not see me actually sliding down the rings, she did notice the wet spots on the back of my jeans. "Miss Popolis, how did you get so wet?"

I thought quickly, but came up with nothing.

"Have you perhaps taken a slide down Neptune's rings?" she asked, her eyebrows raised.

"Yeah," I admitted, slumping down, ashamed.

I wasn't sure, but I think that Mrs. Gophersmocker was holding back a smile. The only way I suspected this was because her eyebrows were twitching. "Don't do anything like that again without permission, Miss Popolis."

Then she really shocked me. "Okay, class. Ava had a good idea. This is a once-in-a-lifetime opportunity! We are going to take a slide on Neptune's rings. Never do this without a partner, as it can be very dangerous. The rings are surprisingly slick and fast so be careful. You may proceed!"

We all stopped our brooms on Neptune's rings and sat down, holding our brooms in our laps. Then we pushed with our hands, and we were off.

We glided down the rings for a little while, but eventually Mrs. Gophersmocker told us that enough was enough. We had to stop now and get back on our brooms. We all had wet backsides, but I think it was worth it. It was super-cool! (*Cool* in both ways!)

When we returned to Dream Ring, the power was back on. This had been the best day at Dream Ring yet!

Chapter Sixteen

The two weeks after Mom's last letter passed in a blur. All of a sudden the first semester was over, and we got our report cards. I was pretty pleased with mine:

DREAM RING, NEPTUNE
First Semester Report Card
Student: Ava Popolis

("NT"=not taken)

Math *(Professor Addsubmerd):* B+

Science *(Professor Lorn):* A

Literature *(Professor Bird):* B

Powers Against Evil Witchcraft *(Professor Gophersmocker):* C

Flying *(Mrs. Gophersmocker):* A+

Musical Magic Against Evil *(Mr. Minaga):* F

Medication Using Magic: NT

Stargazing *(Professor Eleema):* A+

Fortune Telling *(Madam Tralah):* A

Woodworking: NT

Wishful Thinking *(Professor Skids):* B+

Technology with Magic: NT

COMMENTS:

(Flying) *Ava is meant to be in the air. She executes her flying techniques with grace and confidence. Keep it up!*

(Musical Magic) *Ava needs to study more.*

(Wishful Thinking) *Ava shows promise in this area of magic. If she spent more time studying, she could have an A+.*

(Fortune Telling) *Ava always raises her hand in class. And she always pays attention, too. She is a perfect student.*

Headmistress Signature: _____

Parent Signature: _____

Student Signature: _____

Tardy: 4 times

Absent: 0 times

I was satisfied with my report card. I think that some of the teachers exaggerated their comments, and others were too harsh. But overall, I was proud of myself. I had had a pretty good first semester. Maybe not all A's, but learning the basics of magic was hard!

Now I had to explain to my mom why I got an F in Musical Magic Against Evil. (Licklici hadn't agreed with Mom that I should quit.☹) I thought of several techniques:

"Mom, I was so scared of the man, I trembled in his presence and couldn't focus on tests."

"Sorry, Mom, but I was so scared of him that I skipped all of his classes." No, that wouldn't work, since I had no absences.

"Mom, he was just a suckish teacher. I did the best I could."

Or I could tell her the truth: "Mom, he flunked everyone." He seriously did—he gave everyone an F. Some people cried, others laughed, some just stared at their report cards. Some of the desperate ones tried magic to change it. (It didn't work and resulted in a *long* detention.)

The morning after we got our report cards our parents arrived. We were all crowded around the entrance of Dream Ring, waiting. I was so excited; I hadn't seen Mom in five months, and she was almost here!

They arrived right on schedule. Mom was towards the back of the parents, chatting with Victoria's mom. Mrs. Mongrelo was riding on Mom's flying carpet with her, and it looked really cool, gliding through the air.

"Mom!" I hugged her tight when she got off the carpet.

"Oh, Ava. It's so good to see you. I've missed you so much!" Mom had tears in her eyes, and her fingernails flashed red, which I guess means love. I was surprised to see my fingernails glow with a faint red light. My powers were starting to come in!

We ate with our parents in the main hall. Mom and I both wished for the same thing: her amazing pot roast, mashed potatoes, and beets. I hadn't stopped talking with Mom yet. She was dressed in her full witch costume, I guess. [What else can you call it?] She wore a maroon long-sleeved shirt, jeans, and a long white robe that made her face and neck look really tan. Her maroon earrings looked very elegant against her dark blond hair, which she'd pulled back into a French braid. She looked at home on Neptune, which made me wonder if people ever live here, or just professors and students.

After lunch, I showed Mom around our dorm. She gave me some new clothes and toiletries, which I was badly in need of. There weren't any normal grocery stores on Neptune, and I wasn't really old enough to go to them to buy my personal stuff. The thought was just weird.

We just hung out for a while. I took her for a broom ride, and she taught me how to fly her magic carpet. It was a lot more complicated than a broom. If you want to turn right, press the orange rock. Left, press the purple rock. Mom had it down pat, but I had to work at it a while.

I introduced Mom to all my new friends: Ella, Kathryn, Gabriella, and Tanya. Then we headed to the school area of Dream Ring for the parent-teacher conferences. The students were required to attend these, which was a stupid idea, I thought. Why should the students have to sit through the torture of two adults discussing you as if you weren't there?

The parent-teacher conferences were only twenty minutes. Still, that felt like a long time. I mean, I had to sit through *three hours* of parent-teacher conferences. Thank goodness they were spaced out over three days.

The first night we had to meet with Mrs. Gophersmocker, Mr. Minaga, and my Literature teacher, Professor Bird.

"Hello, Mrs. Popolis."

"Mrs. Gophersmocker! So nice to see you again! It's been a while!"

"Yes, dear, it has. We're here to discuss Ava's work, right?"

"Yes. How has Ava done in your class?"

This is when Mrs. Gophersmocker really came alive. "Ava has been a most wonderful student. Superb. She has the most magnificent ideas, both creative and educational. She can be a bit of a troublemaker sometimes, but it often results in people learning, so I am okay with it. She always listens well, and she is never disrespectful. I am very pleased with Ava!"

"Do you have any concerns?"

"Oh, no, Mrs. Popolis. She is a perfect student."

"Is her broom okay?"

"Yes, although sometimes I wonder whether she would do better with something else, maybe a flying carpet. You always had trouble with your broom, as I recall."

"Yes," Mom sighed. "That's why I switched."

"That's right! Well, Mrs. Popolis, I don't have anything left to say. She is a pleasure to have in class."

"Thank you!"

They shook hands and we left.

"Wow, she sure is pleasant," Mom said as we walked to Musical Magic Against Evil.

"Yep."

We walked the rest of the way in silence.

Ten minutes later it was time for our conference with Mr. Minaga.

"Hello, Mrs. Popolis—Lilly, if I may," Mr. Minaga said, quite formally.

"Hello," she said coldly, her demeanor changing from bubbly and warm to withdrawn and frosty in the snap of a finger. Her fingernails turned from a nice shade of maroon to a black as deep as the sky during a thunderstorm on Earth. "So."

"Well, Ava has been the best student I've had this year."

"Really?" Mom sounded skeptical, and I was sure it was because she had seen my report card.

"Nah, I was just joking with you," he said, with an evil grin that suddenly made me feel *very* tired. "She has been a very ill-behaved student. She never studies for tests and I am very disappointed in her behavior." He looked closely at Mom. "Do you have anything to say in response?"

"As a matter of fact, I do," Mom said bravely. She yawned before she said, "Why did you flunk my daughter? She studies and excels in school. She tries hard to be a good student. You were the only teacher who gave her an F. I don't believe she deserves it."

"I understand where you're coming from."

"No, Mr. Minaga, I don't think you do."

Mr. Minaga's eyes flashed red. He stood up and pulled his wand out of his pants pocket, his wand glowing red. He started to say a spell, but Mom cut him off.

"BLIND!" she yelled fiercely. But Mr. Minaga was ready, and had put up a force field. Mom did as well.

"Okay, c'mon!" I said. "This isn't going anywhere. If you both have force fields, then spells will do nothing."

Mr. Minaga's eyes flashed bright red again, and he pointed his wand at me. But I caught him off guard when I took a pencil out of my pocket and yelled "BLIND!" I knew that it wouldn't do anything, but it startled him into staring for a split second. I took that time to grab my mom's arm and run.

We barely escaped. Mr. Minaga fired a spell at us as we left, and the door erupted into flames. Mom and I ran until the cramps in our sides forced us to stop. Then we hugged each other and fell down. My fingernails glowed a faint black, the color for anger, I'm guessing.

"I'm glad *that's* over with!" I said, then laughed feebly. I was shaking, and still really scared. "Mom, you were awesome."

"Thanks, honey. Now let's go. We're almost late for the conference with your Literature teacher, Professor Bird."

"Right. I'll fly you there." So Mom made my broom appear and then I flew her back to the main hall so we could dash to the Literature room.

We got to the conference just in time. Mom led the way into the dimly-lit Literature room. My teacher, Professor Bird, sat in a leather chair behind his expensive-looking desk. His black hair was slicked back with about a tube of hair gel. His pale hands were clasped on top of the desk. "Good evening," he said. "Mrs. Popolis, Ava."

"Hello, Professor Bird. We are here to discuss Ava's grade in Literature."

"Yes. Ava has done very well in my class. A 'B' is a very respectable grade. If she would study a little more or do a couple more assignments she could easily have an 'A.'"

"I see. She hasn't turned in all of her assignments?"

"No. I receive about three-fourths of the homework from Ava. It seems to me that she does not take this subject seriously."

"Not true!" I interrupted. "I studied ver—well, I sorta studied for my tests."

"Yes."

"Ava! I thought we agreed you'd study hard at Dream Ring! This is a school where you need to be serious!" Mom scolded.

"I know. Sorry."

"I expect you to turn in all your assignments in second semester. You got me?"

"Yeah."

"No. You say, 'Yes, Mother,'" Professor Bird told me in a sweet voice.

"Yes, Mother," I said in a fake obedient voice. I was *so* done with all of these conferences. And to think this was just the first night—the thought there were two more to come was almost enough for me to get a detention so that I could skip them.

"Do you have anything more to add, Professor Bird?"

"Yes, Mrs. Popolis. First, I think Ava potentially has a knack for reading or language of some sort. We will start reading a book by the famous Peter Henry Widdidorm, titled <u>Your Powers Come In</u>, and I am interested to see how she does with the vocabulary. Second, I think your dress is very... becoming on you. I think you're beautiful."

"Professor Bird! We are strictly here for school."

Professor Bird opened his mouth to say something, but Mom strode out of the classroom before he could respond.

Chapter Seventeen

The week that Mom stayed on Neptune was the shortest week of the whole time that I had been at Dream Ring. We took a ride on Neptune's rings again, played board games together, and she taught me some spells that I could do without a wand and a few cool moves on my broom. She also taught me a little about how to fly a magic carpet, but I wasn't too good at it yet.

On Saturday Mom had to leave. She wore a black robe over a white tank top and sweatpants. Her fingernails flashed green, which she told me meant jealousy.

"Who are you jealous of?" I asked her.

"Of you," she said, "You get to stay on Neptune."

"Well, I'm jealous, too. Of *you*. You get to go back to the real world."

Mom's face darkened and became very serious. "But, honey, you have to understand—this is a world, too. A world for people like you and me. You're not safe in the real world. After you train, you might be able to come back to Earth for summer vacation, and then you can *move* back to Earth. But for now, Neptune is your home."

I blinked back my tears. I wanted e-mail, I wanted my cell phone, and I wanted my iPod. I wanted to listen to music at home, and to gossip with my friends. I wanted my own room. All of that was home to me, but I couldn't have that. It was so disappointing. I'd been hoping that Mom would be sympathetic and decide that I could fly home with her.

No such luck.

Was there even such a thing as luck on Neptune? I *was* on a different planet, for goodness sakes.

"Bye, Mom," I said. "Love you. Please come and visit soon."

"I'll try. Bye, Ava."

"Bye!" Then Mom left with her witch and wizard friends. They flew up into Neptune's atmosphere and disappeared.

But when I flew back to my dorm, I found one last gift from Mom. My favorite gift.

On my nightstand was a small red box. Inside was a note and a small blue flip-phone. Instead of numbers and texting letters, though, it had six small photos. There were Mom, Dad, Caleb, Victoria, and a blank space. I tried touching Mom's picture, and a voice boomed from the small phone. "Call Mom?" it asked. "YES!" I shouted. A working phone on Neptune!! I was so excited that I jumped up and down.

I heard ringing and then Mom's voice. "Hello?" she said.

"Mom! Thank you so much for the phone! Will it work for *anyone?*"

"Yes. All you do is click the 'OK' button to take a picture of someone. The phone processes it, and then whenever you press the picture, it calls that person. If you don't have the person with you, take a picture of a photograph you may have of them, if that makes any sense."

"'Kay. Still following you."

"You can fit twenty-eight contacts in your phone. If you're full and can't fit another person, delete one by voice command, and add the new contact. Then, after you've called that person, delete his or her picture and put the other person back in. It's easy."

"Who else has one?"

"All freshman students on Neptune get one from their parents after first semester."

"Awesome! But wait, you can call regular people too, right?"

"Yeah."

"Thanks so much, Mom! Gotta go. Bye!"

"Glad you like it! Bye!"

After my phone call with Mom, I called Victoria and Caleb. And, of course, Dad! He sounded relieved to hear from me, and I had to make a split-second decision: whether or not to talk in a European accent! (I didn't.) He talked to me about sports, his work, what was going on at home, and, of course, he asked me how I was doing in Europe. I gave him honest answers, but left most details vague.

It was so good to hear Caleb's sweet southern drawl, and my phone calls left me in a good mood.

The only bad thing about the Neptune phone was that you couldn't text on it, but that was okay with me. I could call anyone I wanted, from *Neptune!* That made things feel a little bit more normal, like I was an almost-regular teenager.

Chapter Eighteen

Shortly after the first semester ended, I started to get a weird headache. It was intermittent, but it was consistently there every day.

I also felt strange. Sometimes my eyes hurt, and sometimes my skin felt wet. Not just sweat, though—it was, like, soaked.

When there was a thunderstorm or any weather different from the usual gray sky, my head hurt even worse.

I called Mom to tell her about my symptoms. She listened with sympathy, but she sounded rushed. "It's okay, honey," she told me. "This time will end soon. You'll get through it."

"What 'time?'" I asked.

"The time you're going through right now. The headaches, the weather."

"Yeah. And Mom?"

"What, honey?"

"Well, my fingers hurt, too."

"Good. Sorry, but I have to go. Bye! I love you!"

I said to myself, "Whatever. That was weird. Really, Mom? 'Good? Sorry? I have to go?' Whatever."

We got two new classes in the second semester, and we were allowed to drop two. I dropped Musical Magic Against Evil and Wishful Thinking. We weren't really supposed to drop Musical Magic, but Mom's letter had convinced Licklici that it was best for me not to take the class any longer. In the first semester, she wasn't convinced, but a second letter from Mom, sent after the conference, got a little extreme. And then Licklici was convinced.

The two new classes we added were Potions and Powers.

My first Potions class was on Tuesday at 10:00 A.M. Normally, I don't like having to get up before ten but this was an exception. I had heard that the teacher was super nice and that her class was really good. I was excited to meet her.

"Hello, everyone. My name is Professor Threcar. I'm a fairy, and my people are from Saturn. We have extremely good healing powers, and that's why I'm your Potions teacher. We will have a good time this year. It will be tough, but fun. I expect your behavior to be exemplary here in the lab. It is very important that you have good etiquette in the lab because if you knock over any of our ingredients, they could be deadly to you and your classmates. I have a husband, but he is back on Saturn. He is also a fairy. Any questions?"

While the nerdy kids asked questions about our daily work, I took the time to evaluate Professor Threcar. She was petite, dainty, and had good taste in clothes. Her honey-colored robes completely covered her neck, torso, and legs. On her feet were gold slippers. Her hair was black as midnight, and it curled in ringlets around her heart-shaped face. Her blue eyes shone brightly. Her voice was high and squeaky, but it was pretty, too, just like the rest of her. She was elegant, as a fairy should be. I had a feeling that she would be a great teacher.

Professor Threcar moved to the blackboard. "For your first assignment, you'll make a simple dry potion. Even though you use no wet items, it will be very strong, so at tasting time, eat only about a teaspoonful. Good?"

"Yes, Professor Threcar," the class chorused.

"Good. I will give you a list of ingredients and the procedure and then I will float around and observe you do your project. Please work in pairs."

I was paired with Victoria, whose eyes were shining. She looked like she was having a good time.

How the heck were Victoria and I supposed to follow these directions?

INGREDIENTS FOR POTOKO:

You will find these ingredients on the floating counter in the center of the room.

1 cup of magic chips

1 cube of compacted dragon toenails

2 jert roots from the magic garden outside the main hall *(What was a jert?)*

8 shredded pinecones from the weeping willow tree *(That didn't make much sense! Pinecones come from **pine** trees.)*

2 sliced beetles. **Make sure you slice exactly through the middle of their eyes; that's the only way the spell will work.**

PROCEDURE:

Put all the ingredients into a big mixing bowl.

Stir thirty-four times to the right.

Say 'ytilibisivni' four times while you stir for twenty-eight seconds to the left.

Use a whisk to beat the mixture for two minutes.

Pour the finished mixture into a jar. Make sure the lid is on tightly.

Shake for fifty-nine seconds.

Say 'ytilibisivni' again seven times.

Open the jar. The color should be greenish-black.

Taste one teaspoonful of the mixture. Each teaspoon that you take will be effective for twenty minutes. Never take over six teaspoons; more will kill you.

"Oh, I just remembered!" the Professor said triumphantly. "This potion is due by the end of class because if you let the ingredients sit for over an hour, they will mold and be unusable. Get to work!"

We collected our materials quickly. A couple of them were really disgusting. Dragon toenails? Sliced beetles? Gross.

And we found out that a *jert* was a magical fruit that looked sort of like a cross between a giant strawberry and a green bean. It's kind of hard to explain.

Victoria and I did the best we could. At the end of class, we were done, and I hoped we'd done it right. I mean, we tried to count the number of times that we stirred, but what if we got it wrong? Would it kill us? If I hadn't trusted Professor Threcar, I wouldn't have tasted it. But I was pretty sure she would never hurt us, so I measured out a teaspoonful of the potion in the jar, cringed, and swallowed it. It was cold and pretty gross, with a tangy taste like cinnamon and sea salt. The nasty taste was nicely spread throughout the potion. Yuck.

I noticed a change in me almost immediately. I couldn't see myself! I was invisible! *This* was going to be useful, I thought. I was going to be invisible for only twenty minutes, so I had to make a quick escape.

Sadly, Professor Threcar was smart. She had put up an invisible barrier around the room. When I slipped out the door, an alarm beeped and the professor came and led me back to class. No escape would take place today, but maybe the walls would be gone by tomorrow.

"Now, students," Professor Threcar said. "When you turn it in, I expect to see all of the potion there. And be informed, we professors can see you, even though you can't see each other when you're invisible. So discard any dreams of escape right now. Understand?"

Since we knew that she could see us, we nodded. "Good. Now, tomorrow we will learn about a potion that gives you complete control over a classmate for about ten minutes. Of course, there is a spell for that, too, but sometimes it's better to use the potion."

"Thank you, Professor Threcar!" we said, and bounded out of the room when the bell rang. I grabbed my broom and flew off to my next class, Powers, all the while chatting with Victoria about how cool that class would be. Hmmm... what would Powers be like? It would need to be a pretty good class to match up to my impression of Potions.

For some reason, Powers class was located all the way on the other end of campus, which was a *long* way. It took our class about thirty minutes to get there by broom. We had been told to bring a notebook, a pen, and our brains. Victoria and I carpooled on my broom; yesterday her broom (Dream Ring was lending her one for the year) went out of whack and kinda dumped her. She wasn't hurt, but it really scared her.

Victoria and I got there a little late because we went the long way, flying out of the atmosphere and into space. Then we took a ride on Neptune's rings. When our bottoms started to go numb, we got off and flew back into Neptune, where we sped to Powers class.

It was a bad, bad decision to take that detour. Our Powers teacher, Professor Dolsiboar, was a real grump. He moaned at us for being late, and gave us detention. I really liked him. We got off to a great start, don't you think? NOT!!

"My name is Professor Dolsiboar," he said. "I am from Earth, Britain to be exact. I hail from London."

This guy was weird. I'm not exactly sure what creeped me out so much, but this dude was odd, in a strange sort of way. His voice was eerie, and he had an almost scary calmness around him.

"I will be your Powers teacher. In this class we will test certain situations to see what powers you have been given. I also want a paper describing any unusual circumstances you have experienced. For instance, some of you have probably endured soakings or icy air around you in the past two weeks. Due Friday. Now, I have some tests to grade, so for the remaining twenty minutes, you may talk quietly with your neighbor."

Victoria and I whispered quietly. "This guy is a creeper!" I whispered. "He freaks… me… out."

"I know!" she said. "He needs to go."

"Right. I'll get to work on that right away." We giggled, because I seemed to have a tendency either to get teachers fired or to make them quit. Could I break Professor Dolsiboar? I would certainly try.

Later, in bed in my dorm room in Yurnia, I thought about the two new classes. They were so different! In one, we made a potion and learned something. In the other, I got detention for being late, and we didn't learn anything. I wished that we could drop another class!

Chapter Nineteen

The next week my powers began to appear quite quickly. Professor Dolsiboar said my headaches and occasional soaking were indications of those powers that were still to be determined. The strange thing was, the man was supposed to be a pro at identifying your powers, but this guy didn't know what powers I would have. He honestly had no clue. Or maybe he was just so busy with our schedule that he couldn't hear me or something.

In class I raised my hand. "Professor Dolsiboar, I had another soaking last night. Are you *sure* you have no idea what powers I may have?"

"In time, dear. Please open your textbooks to Page 17."

"Oh." *Dear?!*

Victoria was having other symptoms of her powers coming in. Her hand muscles hurt, as did her back. Whenever we passed our messengers, they cooed at her. If we passed a dog, it barked;

a cat meowed. And every day, the air surrounding Victoria was colder than ever.

It was weird. We had no idea what was happening to us, what powers we were getting. And Professor Dolsiboar had no time to help his little "dears"—a comment that still disgusts me—to figure it out. We had only a vague idea what we had a chance of getting. A *small* idea.

Even though Professor Dolsiboar had no clue about our powers yet, we did work in his class. We read a textbook about the many types of powers and we wrote papers. We learned the pros and cons of each power, and we had to do one major project researching our family's powers. Throughout my family history, everyone had had Fingernails, so it was pretty obvious I would get that.

"The maximum number of powers anyone can get is three," Professor Dolsiboar lectured one boring Monday morning. "It is not possible to have any more. Now I want you all to write a story about a character who has four powers, and make sure that it has an ending. Minimum of twelve pages. Due Wednesday. Class is dismissed."

We filed out of the classroom. If I wanted enough time to make a phone call before Potions, I'd have to fly at maximum elevation and top speed to my dorm, *and* do an Eggbomb. I was willing to do it, and besides, I seemed to have a knack for flying. And since we learned how to steer, I've been even better. I hadn't fallen off yet, so I took that as a sign that I was a natural.

The only injury that I got from flying fast and dangerous was a headache, but I barely noticed. I had them all the time, so it didn't matter.

"Hello?"

"Yeah. Hi, Mom. How are you?"

"Good. I haven't heard from you in a while. Is everything okay, honey?"

"Yeah. It's good. My powers are coming in, and it's a real pain. Literally. I just wanted to call to check in. I have about five minutes before Potions. I don't think Professor Threcar will mind if I'm a little late, but then again you never know."

"Everything's good here. Would you like to talk to Dad?"

"Yes. Bye, Mom. Love you."

"Bye, sweetie. Love you, too."

There was a long pause.

"Hello?"

"Dad?"

"Baby! I haven't heard from you in a long time. How is everything at your school?"

"Fine! It's a little lonely, but it's mostly pretty good."

"Well good. Your mother tells me that your talents are really blossoming at your school."

"Um, yeah. I guess you could say that."

"You always were so modest."

"Uh. Thanks. Well, sorry, Dad, but I'm going to be late for class if I don't hang up. Love you!"

"Bye, honey. Love you too!"

After that phone call, I honestly wished that I could tell my dad that I was a witch. I hoped that that law would be overruled eventually.

I hung up and ran to class—I didn't have enough time to fly. Besides, I was, like, two minutes from class. Even I could run that far.

In Potions we made a really cool brew that would heal deep gashes or cuts. I had a bruise from tripping on the concrete, and the concoction really made it better. It was amazing.

To state the obvious, I really liked Potions.

But at the end of class, Professor Threcar announced that we were having another hour of Potions. "Instead of making a potion or doing a report, you will be finding out your powers. Licklici said that I may give you a special tonic that will make your powers known. Now, this potion requires complete focus on the potion's drinker, so we need absolute silence in the class. I will call you up alphabetically by your first name. So, Ava, you're first."

I blushed and headed up to the 'stage' that Professor Threcar had set up, and sat on a stool. Professor Threcar gave me a spoonful of a foul-smelling tonic that was pond-scum green. I smelled and scowled. "Just try it, Popolis. Don't be a wimp!" Professor Threcar teased.

I tipped the spoon into my mouth and felt the slimy liquid go into my body. It was utterly disgusting. The crowd "oohed" and "aahed." "What's happening?" I asked them. I couldn't feel anything except a headache that was getting worse by the minute, and the feeling that my arms and legs were completely wet. How embarrassing! Why did I have to have a soaking in front of everyone? I tried to keep my concentration, I really did, but it was hard.

Professor Threcar handed me a mirror, and I screamed in shock. Above my head was a blue cloud that shimmered when I lost my concentration. On the cloud were three words: Fingernails-Weather-Potions. After a minute, the words and cloud disappeared, and my headache relaxed. I willed my body to dry, and magically, it did. I guess my powers were fairly well-established—finally! It was about time!

"Okay. So now we know. What do they mean?" I demanded. All that studying in Powers just went *ka-plow!* out of my brain.

"Well, with Fingernails, your nails change color according to mood."

"I know that!" I snapped. I was surprised at my bad mood. I had felt fine a minute ago. Why was I so agitated?

"With Weather, you can control the weather around you within 150 yards," she said. "And Potions is the the magical knowledge specializing in how to put together a potion in order to make it do what you want."

"Okay, so that's why my head hurt? Because my brain was imagining all the potions I would put together? And my body kept getting me wet because it was sorta making it rain. And my hands hurt because my fingernails were trying to get used to being a show of my moods."

"Sort of," Professor Threcar said uncertainly. "I think so. I've never really done this before," she said. "Well, Brian, it's your turn."

And so it went. My classmates each found out their powers. Victoria had Flower, Animal, and Ice. Flower was the ability to make flowers grow and turn them into magical potions. Animal was the ability to converse with animals. (I don't know why that's a power; it seems stupid to me, but Victoria sure was proud of it. Kinda funny that she got Animal since she's always been so afraid of them.) And Ice was the ability to make water freeze around you. You can freeze people, whole places, or things. Also, you can make the air around you seem really cold.

When we went home, I tried out my powers. I willed it to rain. It sorta did. I mean, I got a couple of sprinkles from the ceiling. My fingernails flashed black. I wasn't sure I liked the whole Fingernails thing. I mean, sometimes you don't want people to know what you're feeling, you know?

Chapter Twenty

On Thursday morning I woke up to a loud bell ringing incessantly—it just went *'DING, DING, DING!'* I willed it to stop. I even tried whispering spell-like rhymes at the bell, but it wouldn't stop. All the girls in my dorm were covering their ears and trying to go back to sleep.

Then a loud voice boomed above the bell. "Good morning, students! Please get dressed as usual for your classes, but instead of breakfast in the dorm, report to the main hall. You must be there by 9:30. For those of you who don't know, it is 8:45." The voice ended, as did the bells. My whole dorm breathed a sigh of relief. My fingernails flashed yellow, which I've figured out means I'm irritated. Victoria breathed deeply, and I swear, the room temperature decreased by, like, ten degrees. "Sorry!" she said. "I can't control these things yet."

"It's okay," Gabriella said, "I've got Heat." She breathed out an equivalent sigh, and the room went back to normal.

"That's gonna be useful," I remarked as I dressed in my usual maroon sweatpants, white T-shirt, flip-flops, and gold earrings. It was kinda cold today, so I slipped on the University of New Hampshire hoodie that I got for Christmas.

We all reported to the main hall just a few minutes before the bell rang again, just three short '*DINGs.*'

"Good morning, everyone," Licklici said, looking elegant and beautiful, as usual. "We are gathered for some very important news." She paused so that we could stop talking and focus solely on what she was saying. "I don't really know how to break this to you. Professor Dolsiboar was released yesterday. We felt that he was not fulfilling his position, and that there was a better teacher for your Powers class. So Professor Threcar will be your Powers *and* Potions teacher. When you have your Powers class, just go to Professor Threcar's classroom instead of Professor Dolsiboar's old classroom. Any questions?"

There were none, so we ordered breakfast, eating quickly before going to our classes.

"Oh. My. Gosh!" I said to Victoria as we flew to our first class. "This is AWESOME!"

"I know! He's *gone!* And better, you didn't even have to break him!"

"I feel like a weight has lifted. I mean, he was possibly the worst teacher on Ear—Neptune!" We laughed and Eggbombed onto the carpet outside the entrance to Literature class.

Literature was the same. Since the conferences, Professor Bird has been asking after my mother. I know he likes her, which seems totally weird. My dad is the only person that I can imagine with Mom!

The rest of the day was boring and the same. I was beginning to get restless. When could I get back to Earth? I was beginning to crave a… yep, you guessed it, *mall*.

Chapter Twenty One

I was seriously restless the whole rest of the week. And by Saturday I had my bags packed.

"Where are you going?" Victoria asked me Saturday evening, eyeing my suitcase and broom lying side-by-side on my bed.

"Nowhere," I lied.

"Doesn't look like nowhere to me," she said. "I have my eye on you."

Great. Now I couldn't escape.

Victoria kept me close the whole weekend. She didn't leave my side. We wrote letters, played games, played with our messengers, joked, talked, and took midnight rides on our brooms, higher than we were allowed to go. She knew I was restless to go home, but she wouldn't give in to my endless begging for her to cover for me while I escaped.

"Okay, so I feel the same way," she told me. "I'm craving a mall, and Mom's homemade cheesecake, and all things yummy and Earthly. But we can't go home! You know my mom. If I returned to Earth without permission or good reason, then I would be grounded like I've never been grounded on Earth before. I want to go, you know, I really do. I'm as fidgety as you are. But *we can't go home.*"

"Maybe you can't," I argued. "But I can. I'll risk the disappointment of my parents. Please just look the other way and let me go!" I missed being in my own room, going to the pool with my friends to cool down in the summer, and seeing Dad. I hadn't seen him in nearly a year, and it was almost driving me insane. I just really needed something familiar in my life at that moment.

"No. Because if you left, then what would I do? Best friends can't survive on their own. And what about Widdidorm—think about it, Av. If he saw you traveling *alone* in the *solar system,* don't you think he would take what was laid out for him on a silver platter?"

That got me stuck—I hadn't really thought about Widdidorm in the jumble of everything. "I know. I'm sorry. I'm just ready for a vacation."

"Totally understood. Now, what do you say we go raid the kitchen for some mega-huge ice cream sundaes? You know you love the way I make 'em!"

I giggled and followed her, where she proceeded to make her top-secret sundae. It was scrumptious. For the moment, my need for home was fulfilled. The funny part is, I wasn't truly home, but it felt like old times on Earth.

I survived for about another week before trying to leave again. This time I was serious. I was tough. I was ready to go home, and nothing was going to stop me!

"Just stay one more day, Ava," Victoria pleaded with me. "And then I guess you're free to go."

I owed her that much, so I agreed to stay one more day.

"Ahh… " I sighed. Today was my last day. I stretched awake and looked around. I would come back after a month or so. I mean, I couldn't last too long without Victoria. Maybe I could convince her to come with me. Then I need never return.

"Good morning, students!" Licklici's cheerful voice filled the dorm from the invisible speaker. "Today is our annual field trip! You will need to pack your broom and a change of clothes just in case you need them. No cell phones, please, or electronics. After you're packed, bring your suitcase and broom and WALK to the main hall. You will break into groups and we will begin our field trip. Good?"

I sprang out of bed. This was a good omen, to stay one more day and then leave. I would get to go on the famous field trip and then leave. Perfect!

I followed Licklici's orders and headed to the main hall with Victoria, who was eyeing me and my broom, making sure I wasn't trying to escape. (Which I wasn't!)

At about 9:00 A.M. we departed from Dream Ring. We flew about three-quarters of the way around Neptune before finally landing. Which, knowing that Neptune is like the fourth-biggest planet by diameter in the solar system, takes quite a long time.

"Here we are!" Licklici said excitedly. "Our famous field trip!"

Mom had told me about the field trip and explained where we would go, but I had forgotten all about it. Like amnesia; it had all been swept out of my mind. Weird. I got the feeling it wasn't just forgetfulness. Did Licklici and a spell have something to do with this?

I looked around at where we had landed. It was just like the rest of Neptune: beautiful landscapes, but colder, which made it feel dismal, even though it was amazingly pretty. I don't know how it was possible, given such little sunlight, but there were patches of pastel-colored wildflowers all around us. There were stalks of long grass that smelled nice and outdoors-y, and the clouds were fluffy and bouncy-looking. It was just a field, with some trees on the border. Nothing special. In fact, nothing at all. But it was beautiful nothing-ness.

I seriously think that place was the middle of nowhere.

Had Licklici lost her mind?

"Um, Licklici," I tried, but she cut me off.

"We are here for the field trip that first-years take right after they discover their powers. In the second semester, you will start learning spells. A few of you already know some, but this year's lessons will focus mainly *on* spells.

"During this field trip, you will get your wand."

The whole first-year class chattered excitedly. Wands! I had wondered when we would get them.

"Class of Yurnia, please step forward carrying your brooms."

We stepped forward.

"You will be going first."

Going where? I wondered. Like I said, this was literally the middle of nowhere.

"Mrs. Gophersmocker and Professor Threcar will escort you."

Well, at least we had the good teachers.

"Come on, look alive now, follow your teachers. I will see you soon."

Mrs. Gophersmocker and Professor Threcar led us into the woods about a quarter of a mile away from the field. It was even colder there because no sunlight reached us. I zipped up my jacket.

We stopped when we reached a great tree, at least five feet in diameter. Its limbs were really thick and gnarled, and it must have been at least a thousand years old. I reached out and touched it. The bark was surprisingly smooth, as if millions of hands had touched this tree.

"Step back," Professor Threcar warned everyone.

She snapped her fingers and muttered something, and a huge scar appeared on the tree, long and in the shape of a large "D." Mrs. Gophersmocker withdrew her wand from her robe; it was long, smooth oak, with a reddish tinge to it. She traced the scar on the tree with her wand in a deliberate manner, obviously being careful what strokes she made on the tree. The inside of the "D" disappeared, leaving a wide hole.

"Who wants to go first?" Professor Threcar asked enthusiastically. "It's not a bad fall."

We all stared at the ground covered in dead leaves and moss.

Please don't pick me. Please don't pick me. Please don't pick me…

"Miss Ava, you seem to be a pretty brave girl. How about you go first?"

"Um, no, that's okay."

"Really, I insist. You are such a good student; this is like a reward."

"Uh, no thanks."

"Miss Popolis!" Mrs. Gophersmocker's voice was as sharp as a tack. "You will follow your teacher's orders."

"Yes, ma'am."

I stepped closer to the hole and felt around with my foot. I found just emptiness.

"We will meet you down there. Really, it is a soft landing."

"Great to know."

"Jump, Ava, then shift into an Eggbomb and fly down." Mrs. Gophersmocker's voice was hard and strained.

I hesitated.

And she pushed.

I quickly shifted into an Eggbomb. The little space inside the tree trunk was small, so I was basically falling vertically. I fell for like, a minute before hitting the ground. For a minute, I was dazed. Where was I? Then I got my bearings, and picked up my broom.

It was dark underground. I tried to cast some sort of spell for light or sunshine, but it didn't work. The only light that I could see was about a half-mile up a gravelly road. It was rocky underneath my feet, and I just kept following the path until I reached the light. It gave just enough of a glow for me to read the sign that hung on the small building:

DARREN'S WANDS

it read in shaky letters, grayed with age. (That explains why the scar was in the shape of a "D.") I wasn't really sure what was behind the door—and I sure didn't want to find out alone—so I decided to wait for my other classmates and teachers before going in. I was scared, alone in the pitch-black. It was, like, twenty minutes before I even saw another human being, and by then I was on the verge of a panic attack. How I could see them a half mile away in pitch-blackness, I don't know, either. Then it took that person, like, another fifteen minutes to walk down the gravel road. I was just glad to see another human being.

"Victoria!" I shouted when I saw her. That was a mistake. Underground, on Neptune, my voice really carried—right into Darren's Wands.

"Who are you?" A deep, deep voice sounded from the store. I sorta recognized that voice, but I couldn't place it. It had been several weeks since I had heard it.

Victoria and I looked at each other, and I knew that her face was a mirror of mine—faces of fear.

My fingernails flashed dark blue, which I had come to recognize as fear.

"Should we run?" I whispered very quietly.

She shrugged. Vic never was very handy in tough situations.

Then she shocked me. Victoria held her head up high and walked into Darren's Wands.

"What are you *doing?*" I hissed.

She just opened the door and marched into the building, and I had no choice but to follow her.

"Hello, ladies. Yurnian first-years," he sneered. I looked into the man's face. He wore a long black robe that fully covered him from his neck down. His long black hair just touched his shoulders, and his eyes were gray and hard. His lips stayed curved in a sneer. His speech included a funny accent, maybe Russian. I couldn't tell.

A horrid smell filled the air. It smelled like one of the potions I made that had failed beyond conversation. I wanted to sleep very badly, and I fought the urge to close my eyes and curl up on the floor.

I had to fight the sleepy feeling and get rid of Mr. Minaga—his was the voice I had recognized, but hadn't been able to place. But how?

Just then I was saved, as Mrs. Gophersmocker walked in, along with two other first-years.

"Hello, Darren," she said to the long-haired man, the one with the accent.

"Hello, Grace," he returned, sneering a little less.

"These four will be your first customers," she said, turning to us. "I'm going to sit by our fellow professor, Mr. Minaga."

"James Minaga. A great friend of mine," the long-haired Russian man said.

"He is here to protect our students from any danger."

Yeah, right. I seriously believe that's the reason he's here. "To protect the students." Suuuure.

Before she took a seat, Mrs. Gophersmocker whispered in my ear. "Are you all right, Ava? You look funny."

"I'm so tired." She gave me a funny look, then walked away.

Mr. Wanida—the long-haired man who always had a funny look on his face—("Call me Darren,"—as if I would *ever* do that) led us into a smaller room off to the left. As I passed Mr. Minaga, I again strongly felt the need to sleep.

Inside the room were thousands of shoeboxes with labels on them. Some of the labels were funny. Like, "Oak, mealworm wing." Mealworms don't have wings, so what the heck did the label mean? Things sure were weird on Neptune.

"You will go first, dear," Mr. Wanida said in his funny accent. "What is your name?"

"Ava, sir," I said.

"Ah, yes, Ava Popolis. You will make a great decision. But that's later, in your third or fourth year," Mr. Wanida proclaimed solemnly. I really didn't feel like he was authorized to make such a prophecy, but whatever. This man was very strange. I mean, not having sunlight at all, ever, could make you kind of wacky, right? I thought I'd read that somewhere.

"Ohhhh-kay," I said. "Sure."

He glared at my sarcasm and disrespect and silently grabbed my arm. I wrestled out of his grasp. He was trying to lead me to the center of the room, where there was a big lazy Susan-type-thing. Kind of like a big merry-go-round without railings. It was flashing different colors, along with my fingernails. What was happening?

Mr. Wanida snapped his fingers, and a metal bar shot across the gigantic lazy Susan. I jumped out of the way so that it wouldn't go right through my stomach and spear me like a shish kebab. "Hold on," he snarled.

I considered not holding on, but then I decided that Mr. Wanida probably knew what he was doing. I clenched the metal bar with a death grip, and once my hands touched the bar, it started spinning, like, really fast. I held on even tighter.

Suddenly, it stopped spinning. I let go and dropped to the platform like a leaf.

Mr. Wanida grabbed hold of me and dragged me over to the cluster of shoeboxes that I had been facing when that crazy thing finally stopped spinning. He led me onto another sort of platform.

"Oh, no," I said, leery of the platform. "What does *this* thing do?"

"Do you want a wand or not?" Mr. Wanida growled. His accent grew even heavier when he growled, if you can believe *that*. And I thought it was as Russian as you could get when he just talked in his normal voice.

When I hesitated to get on the blue platform that was rapidly changing colors (just like the lazy Susan), the creepy Russian dude lifted me onto it. Yes, I did say LIFTED. He just picked me up and transported me to the platform.

A metal bar shot out again, and I gripped this one so tight that my knuckles turned white. I'm pretty sure that my face was the same color, while my nails were still dark blue.

But the platform started at a very slow, calm pace. I relaxed and started to smile again. It ground to a stop when we reached the first shelf of shoeboxes.

"Hold out your hand," Mr. Wanida commanded. This all sounded like hocus-pocus to me, but I did as instructed.

Nothing happened, so the platform raised another shelf-level.

"Do it again."

I did. Again, nothing happened.

We repeated this five times. By that time, my hand was just below the ceiling.

"Again."

This time, when I put out my hand, a shoebox flew into my hand. One of the corners pierced my hand, and I whimpered. I held the shoebox with both hands, but that was definitely a mistake. The platform shot down as fast as the gigantic lazy Susan thing had spun. I lost my balance and fell onto the platform and I'm pretty sure my spine cracked in half. I felt jolted, dizzy, and still extremely drowsy. The thought crossed my mind that this field trip was *not* all it was cracked up to be. I half-smiled at my ill humor, rubbing my sore back.

"Hmm… " Mr. Wanida said, and inspected the label. "Oak, with a vein of maple, robin feather, and—how interesting—a dragon's horn."

A dragon's horn?

"Well, try it out. Point at me and say, 'Wing-kah-pah,' okay?"

This, too, sounded like hocus-pocus, but I said it anyway. I took my wand in my right hand, pointed it at him, and said, "Wing-cape-uh!" just like he told me too. But something went horribly wrong. Mr. Wanida slowly shrunk down until he was about as tall as my knee.

"What happened?" I asked, panic rising in my voice. "Did I do it right?"

"No!" a shrill Russian voice sounded somewhere near the floor. "But your wand works."

I fought the urge to laugh. How had I managed to turn Mr. Wanida into a midget?

"What did I do wrong?"

"You pronounced it wrong. Go get Mrs. Gophersmocker."

I slunk out of there quickly and found Mrs. Gophersmocker. She gasped when she saw how little Mr. Wanida was. "I shrunk Mr. Wanida," I said, shrugging. "I pronounced my spell wrong."

Luckily Mrs. Gophersmocker was able to get him back to normal height. He was slightly rumpled, but I also think he got some humor out of it. "Congratulations. You got your wand," he said to me in a boring tone, as if he said this to every customer, whether he liked it or not.

Before I could thank him for his help, he snarled, "Now get out of here!" I nodded quickly and strode out of Darren's Wands, hopefully never to return. Before I got out of there, though, Mr. Minaga gave me one piercing look which clearly meant: *I can't wait until I have permission from Widdidorm to kill you.* I don't know how I knew, but that is exactly what he meant, and it really scared me, as I'm sure you can imagine.

I kept walking until I came to what looked like the tree I had been sent down in. I traced a D on the tree with my wand, but nothing happened. My fingernails flashed yellow, for irritated.

I sat down underneath the tree and waited until Victoria, Mrs. Gophersmocker, and the other two girls came back.

The three girls were all carrying new wands, too, and we admired them while Mrs. Gophersmocker got the magic door to open. Then we rocketed up. The hard part about this was that we had been taught only to straddle the broom when doing an Eggbomb, so we had to sit on it sideways while going straight up. If we had been in a normal place we would have fallen straight off, but we somehow made it to the top. Then Professor Threcar took four other girls down. They kept doing that for what seemed like hours. The whole time the rest of us just talked and whipped our wands around, hoping to make something happen.

Finally all of the first-years from Yurnia had their wands. We went back to the Talania students, Licklici, and the other teachers, and waited while they went to the tree and started doing the same process we had been through.

✺

While the Talania students were getting their wands, we got to mess around with ours. Mine was a little over a foot long and had a reddish tinge to it. It was wooden and sturdy. Professor Threcar explained that we had to keep our wands with us at all times in a robe pocket. The robes that I had bought at the beginning of the school year had a pocket just under my right hip, so I stored it there. I wasn't so cold any longer, so I had traded my jacket for my robe, which I had stored in the cellar of my broom. (Hey, if I'm gonna be a witch with a real wand, I might as well look more witch-y.)

Professor Threcar showed us a hidden garden that we had not seen on the way to the tree, and explained its purpose. "These vegetables and fruits are not harvested, so students are allowed to whip their wands around and see what happens. Go ahead, try it."

We eagerly took out our wands and walked over to the garden, which was overgrown with weeds and didn't look like anything important. I waved my wand in front of me and said something that I thought sounded magical. A light shot out of my wand, leaving my hand with a satisfying *zap*, and a watermelon enlarged into a nice size. I laughed out loud and pointed the enormous melon out to Victoria. "No fair!" she insisted, laughing, and tried harder to make something come out of her wand.

We played around for a long time in the garden until the Talania students came back with their wands. Playing in the garden had taken the edge off of the scary trip to Darren's Wands and back.

The Talania group only got a couple of minutes to play in the garden with their new wands, but rumors had been spreading that they had played extreme broom tag while we were gone. Extreme broom tag was one of the greatest magical games that existed on Neptune. I was a little jealous because normally extreme broom tag was against the rules at Dream Ring, and we only get to play it on very special occasions.

We headed home shortly after, arriving two hours after dark. It had been a little boring in spots for the Big Famous

Field Trip, as it was known as, but still fun. But Mr. Wanida
was a creep, and I wasn't going back. The only part that I had
actually enjoyed was playing in the garden. The rest—well,
I wondered why it was so famous. It hadn't seemed all that
monumental to me.

Chapter Twenty Two

The next week, we worked on spells. It took a little while for me to get used to my wand and saying gibberish out loud, but it's pretty fun. I love being able to do things like bring an object to me, or make it disappear, or blind somebody temporarily with my wand. I realized then that this was why the field trip was so important—wands were, like, *necessary* to a witch or wizard!

In Fortune Telling we learned how to make somebody snap into a trance for 30 seconds and tell us exactly what he or she was thinking. I don't really approve of this spell because I think it's cruel. Madam Tralah tried it out on Gabriella, from the Purple Flying Monkeys. Madam Tralah had directed Tanya to do the spell. What she was thinking was kinda sad.

"Derreadin!" Tanya shouted, pointing her wand at Gabriella, who was her best friend.

Gabriella snapped into a trance, her eyes going blank, her limbs spontaneously at attention. "Okay, so I was, like, calling my mom yesterday, and she was, like... and then did you see Zach yesterday? His eyes were as blue as ever, and I swear he looked at me. Then I blushed, and I swear he caught me looking. Okay, so lately Tanya has been really annoying. I can't believe that she also has a crush on Zach; I mean he's totally mine. Like *duh*! And then tonight I have to make dinner and that is such a *drag*."

When she snapped out of it, she blushed. "Uh-oh," she said. "Was it bad?" Madam Tralah actually nodded.

Zach and Tanya were both blushing. Since nobody else was going to say anything to break the tension, Josh said, "Okay, that was awkward." We all laughed nervously. I hoped that none of my friends would use that one on me. It was *not* a good spell. It felt like something that Widdidorm would make, or at least somebody like his kind. I mean, Widdidorm is a lot worse than that; to him, making up a mean spell is *nothing*.

In Stargazing, Professor Eleema taught us a spell that would make the moon and stars look a lot closer. "Couldn't we just fly above Neptune to look at them?" Kathryn asked. Professor Eleema blushed like she hadn't been expecting that question.

"Yes, but sometimes that's not possible," she recovered. "So I'm going to teach you a spell for it." She went on to teach us the spell—which I thought was really dumb. But I pretended to listen and be interested because that's how I had got an A+ in the first semester.

But in Powers Against Evil Witchcraft, we learned the good spells. Our teacher was Professor Gophersmocker, Mrs. Gophersmocker's husband. He was really funny and a great teacher, and he tag-teamed with Professor Threcar to make a really good Spell class. "This is the fun class," he announced on Wednesday morning. It was about 11:00 A.M. and I really wished that I was still sleeping. Why did school have to start so early? My earliest class that day had been at, like, 8:45. I was groggy and tired.

Some of my nerdy classmates cheered. I was excited too; a fun class when we learned spells? Heck, yeah, that was exciting!

"So, if you're in a situation when you find your opponent stronger than you and you decide to abandon the fight, you point your wand at the person and yell 'Blind!' and the person will be temporarily blinded. He or she will fall to the floor, and that's your chance to ditch. I'm going to try it out on Professor Threcar. Everybody watching?"

We all said we were.

"BLIND!" Professor Gophersmocker pointed his wand and yelled at Professor Threcar. She fell to the floor, not faking, actually blinded, and Professor Gophersmocker faked running out of the room. In about a minute, Professor Threcar could see again and we all clapped.

"Okay, kids, pair up and try it out. When you have each successfully done it once, I want you to put your head on your desk. Okay?"

"Sure," we responded.

I paired up with Ella, the red-haired girl that slept next to me. "Blind!" I said, pointing at her with my wand. My wand glowed blue at the tip and Ella fell back. Her head just grazed the back of the desk as she fell, but she appeared to be okay. The spell had worked, too.

A minute later it was my turn. Ella did the spell right, and she knocked me down with her wand. I fell backward, breaking my fall with my wrist. I shouldn't have done that, I thought a split-second later. I couldn't see at all, but I could still feel, and my wrist hurt like the devil. A minute later, when my sight returned, I was still feeling jolts of pain. I tried to shake it off, but it hurt pretty badly.

"The next spell that we'll learn is one when you levitate a person or object. Now, this is a little hard, so it might take a couple of tries. It's harder to get things with more weight off the ground, so maybe just try levitating a light object, like your pen or your hat," Professor Gophersmocker said.

"I'll take it from here. Now, in order to do this spell, you say 'Wing-kah-pah,'" Professor Threcar instructed. She pointed her wand at Professor Gophersmocker, said "Wing-kah-pah," and he immediately rose a couple of feet into the air. I was suddenly glad that this classroom had a high ceiling because I didn't want to risk any accidents.

We practiced this spell with our partners. Seconds before we started, Professor Gophersmocker said, "Oh, and kids? The more you concentrate, the higher the person goes. If you lose your concentration, then the person will plummet back to the ground. So be careful."

That made me just a *little* nervous. I mean, I couldn't stay focused very long, and the pain in my wrist kept distracting me. I didn't want to *hurt* Ella!

"Wing-kah-pah," she said, and I started rising into the air. She kept her focus until I was about ten feet in the air, when she became distracted by a pink paper clip a couple of desks away. The tip of her wand tip stopped glowing, and before I knew it, I was falling back to the cold, cement floor of the classroom. This would not be pretty.

I screamed in pain as I hit the floor, breaking my fall with the wrist that was already injured. The floor was cold and hard and the the pain was too much to bear. I wished that I could pass out—anything was better than feeling this pain—but I wasn't a queasy person who fainted easily.

Professor Threcar was the first to reach me. She cried out when she saw my wrist. I assume it looked very broken, and I felt tears spring to my eyes. This was too much! And I disliked Ella even more now.

(Let me rephrase that: Ella wasn't my best friend before, but we were 'okay' friends. But now—I felt like I couldn't trust her anymore!)

When I tried to look at my damaged wrist, Professor Threcar temporarily blinded me. It felt good to close my eyes, to tell the truth. Next thing I knew, I was being scooped up by, and transported in the arms of, a very nice-smelling man. I was glad

I was blinded because I could dream that this nice-smelling person was somebody other than—Professor Gophersmocker. What a treat. Not!

He carried me to the infirmary where Nurse Norah treated me with a spell that healed my wrist in, like, three seconds. She just basically snapped her fingers, and the pain was gone.

So when the pain left, I hopped up from the infirmary bed. "Thanks, Nurse Norah!" But when my feet hit the floor, I fell over right away.

"Miss Popolis," Nurse Norah said sharply. "You are not to get out of bed for the night. The spell I used to heal your wrist bones was very powerful. It will affect your limbs and you will literally be quite useless. It's much better that you just lie in bed until the full effects are gone. I'm sure your friends will be by soon to visit you."

She was right.

"Are you okay?" Victoria exclaimed when she saw me lying in the hospital bed, my wrist on an ice pack.

"Yes. No. Sort of." She and four others (Tanya, Kathryn, Ella, and Gabriella), sat down in chairs by my bed, and I told them what Nurse Norah had just relayed to me.

"Too bad," they sympathized with me. "The first football game is tonight." There were a grand total of four football teams at Dream Ring, about the only Earth-like thing on this planet, and the first game was tonight.

"I'll be out in a minute. Wait outside the infirmary for me. And be prepared to support my entire body," I instructed like a drill sergeant.

"Ohhhh-kay," Victoria said, giving me the what-are-you-up-to? best friend look. I shot her a look back that I hoped said 'you'll see.' When she walked out she seemed unconvinced.

Nurse Norah entered a couple of minutes later. Right when she came in, I pointed my wand and yelled, "Blind!" just like I was taught. She was momentarily blinded, and I took that time to properly fall out of bed. I dragged myself to the door, stood up long enough to open it, and fell into Victoria and Tanya's arms. They caught me and held me steady while I closed the door and caught my breath. Then they helped me back to Yurnia, where we blinded Yurnia's guard, Amber, too, and hopped into our dorm room.

I knew it was wrong to blind Amber and Nurse Norah, but frankly, I *had* to go to the football game. Everyone was going to be there and a night in the infirmary would be boring. I would go back there for bedtime, but I had to see the game. It was 7:30, and the game started at 8. I had just enough time to freshen up and fly over to the small stadium.

I grabbed a cute outfit and my cosmetic bag and hobbled into the bathroom, managing to fall over several times (I was still a little—make that a *lot*—unstable!). Then I changed into my outfit: jeans, black ankle boots, and a blue tank top. The tank top would be cold, but it matched my eyes to a T. Plus I would stand out—I mean, I would be the only girl whose shoulders were showing!

After slipping on bracelets and a ring, I crimped my hair and put a clip in it. I slipped some hoop earrings in, and then put on a little lip-gloss and some mascara. Perfect! A little perfume, and I was ready.

But as I was walking out, common sense returned, and I grabbed my blue hoodie that *almost* matched my eyes. I slipped it over my head, being careful not to mess up my hair. Then I waited on my bed until Victoria and Tanya were done. They came in and I put my arms on theirs to steady myself.

"Bye, Amber!" we called as we walked out the invisible door of Yurnia. "We'll be at the football game."

The guard eyed me. Uh-oh.

"Please don't tell. You were a freshman once, too. I'm going back to the infirmary for the night. This is just a little outing."

Our quirky guard gave us a thumbs-up to tell us our secret was safe with her. As long as none of our teachers attended the football game, we would be home free.

The football game was a blast, and eventually the spell wore off, so I wasn't tripping like an idiot. The game was actually a ton of fun to watch, too. The boys who played ranged from second-years all the way up to seniors. I couldn't wait until the next game. And after all of the excitement, the infirmary bed didn't feel too bad, either.

Chapter Twenty Three

In the infirmary that night, around 3:45 A.M., I had another meeting with Widdidorm. I'd been tossing and turning, trying to get comfortable, and all of a sudden, I began to feel very, very drowsy. I thought it was just the medicine Nurse Norah had given me at three, but then I realized I'd had this sleepiness before. (Don't ask me why I was still awake then—I just hadn't felt tired at all tonight—until now!)

At least this time I owned a wand. Last time I hadn't—back on Earth—and it hadn't gone well.

I slipped off into the darkness, almost scared to death about seeing Widdidorm again. He was not my pal, my BFF, just the opposite, and I had no idea why. It almost seemed like he wanted to kill me, instead of just harm me, which I couldn't understand at all. I mean, I couldn't understand why he would want to hurt me in the first place, but to *kill* is a little extreme!

In this sleepy state I met him in the hall outside the secret entrance to Yurnia. It was dark, and nobody was around, not even Amber. I was crouched underneath a shelf. He couldn't see me, and so I was safe for a couple minutes. I caught my breath and steadied myself, racking my brain for spells. I remembered one that you could do without your wand—after checking my robe pocket, it was nowhere to be found, and I was trying not to panic. It would bring any magical item to you. I didn't know if it would work in dreams, or whatever this was, but I aimed to try. Softly I said, "emgnirb wand." All of a sudden, there was a soft glow of light, and it whisked into my hand. My wand was here.

That had worked pretty well, so I did it again, this time for a special potion. "Emgnirb Potoko." It took a little longer, but eventually a couple of teaspoonfuls came whisking into view. I had the Invisibility Potion! I sniffed it, and then quickly drew my nose back. Yep, it was definitely Potoko; it smelled and tasted as disgusting as before!

I wished for this dream or encounter or whatever I was in with Widdidorm to start and be done quickly, but to no avail. Eventually, I ran out of Potoko. For some reason Widdidorm kept me waiting longer than forty minutes! I had no idea why, and I was getting desperate. What was I going to do? I couldn't do very many spells a day because my body was still getting used to my powers. I was already exhausted from doing so many spells today.

"Ava." Widdidorm's cold voice rose out of the pitch-blackness. "Come out, or I will hurt you." From any other person I would have laughed, but we're talking about the greatest evil sorcerer in history here! And he was threatening to hurt me, so I showed myself real quick. I was about fifty feet away from him, near the entrance to Yurnia, and he was at the other end of the hall, watching me with cold eyes.

"Ah, yes, Ava Popolis."

I was silent.

"Call me Master!" he demanded.

"I'm sorry. Master."

"That's better. Ava, I'm going to make you very sorry. Now get up."

Okay. I was just stalling for time now. What was I going to do? I knew that I didn't have the strength to fight him, physically or spell-wise.

Suddenly he strode toward me and grabbed me. His fingers were cold and clammy; he was right in front of me. My arm burned where he had touched me, though the hand was cold.

He thrust his face in front of mine, forcing me to look into his cold, hateful eyes. They glowed red and I wasn't sure that he was human anymore.

"Someday you will know, Ava," he hissed. *"Someday you will know."*

I woke up in the infirmary, sweating so much the bed was soaked. I started crying. *What* would I know? And why didn't anybody else have meetings with Widdidorm?

I stood up on shaky legs—not from the healing spell, but from sheer nervousness and fatigue—and grabbed my broom. Walking out the door, I found I was getting a little bit more steady on my legs—which was a great sign, considering the fact that I totally hate being away from my friends and all the action. I took a ride to clear my head. I sure hoped that I didn't meet Widdidorm in person anytime soon!

The next day, I got a letter from Mom. Violet looked very tired and not herself, so I made her a potion that I knew would heal her. It worked like a charm, or should I say, potion. These powers will definitely come in handy.

Dear Ava,

How are you? I feel like I never hear from you anymore. Are you doing all right? Have you seen him again?

Love, Mom

Dear Mom,

Him? Do you mean Widdidorm? If so, then the answer is YES. I had a very real dream-encounter very early this morning, and he told me, 'Someday you will know.' It was all weird. What am I going to know?

Sorry I haven't written. We've been really busy learning new spells.

I broke my wrist when I tried to break my fall in Powers Against Evil Witchcraft. Nurse Norah healed it and I'm all better. Seriously, Mom. I know you're thinking that I'm just saying that, but really, I'm good. Honestly.

Love, Ava

Dear Ava,

Yes, 'him' is Widdidorm. I knew him back at Dream Ring, but I can't say much.

You broke your wrist?! Are you okay? Are you sure? Please be more careful next time.

Did you like the field trip?

Love, Mom

I missed Mom and Dad, but not as I had before the field trip. Now, I want to be here. I want to be learning spells and cool flying tricks. Sure, I still crave a mall every once in a while, but the need to be on Earth had eased a lot. I know that I need to learn more about fighting if I want to live to my twenties.

Later that day, I was discharged from the hospital with a strict order to be pretty laid-back until I felt completely well. Like that would ever happen!

Chapter Twenty Four

The next day, when I was back in the dorm, Licklici made an announcement. "Attention, students! We will be dining in the main hall tonight! Please arrive promptly at 7:00. Thank you!"

A dinner! Victoria and I talked about the reason for it while we dressed and got ready for the day. Today I had Stargazing, Powers and Literature.

I had to hurry to get ready because Literature was at 9:00, a record early time to have this class. Half asleep, I slipped on a T-shirt and sweatpants and put on my longest robes to hide my casual wear. They felt warm and cozy, especially because the weather outside was cold, dreary, and gray.

In Literature we were reading a book about the history of Dream Ring. It was boring and I was so warm that I almost fell asleep. As my eyes rolled back in my head I leaned onto the desk to buckle down for some needed rest. But it was cold and slimy! Or at least, it felt that way. I reeled back, my eyes open wide.

I was awake now! I bent down to examine the desk, but it didn't appear slimy, and it was normal temperature.

I discussed my weird experience as Victoria and I walked to Stargazing. Normally we had class after sunset so that we could actually *gaze* at the stars. But today we were having a daytime lesson, which meant reading a textbook for forty-five minutes. Boring!

"I think," Victoria said slowly, "Bird put a No-Sleep charm on the desks. He's pretty smart."

Sadly, I agreed.

After Stargazing and lunch, we had a short break, only an hour. During that time, I studied for an upcoming Math test. I didn't get the point of studying fractions and decimals if you were a witch, but obviously Licklici and Professor Addsubmerd, (my dorky math teacher), did.

The only interesting thing about my day (other than dinner, which I knew would be fun) was Potions. The topic of discussion was what would happen today in Potions? I told everyone that I thought today we'd be learning a new recipe, Victoria guessed pop quiz, and some kid guessed field trip.

Well, we were all wrong.

"Today we will all be taking a special potion concocted by myself," Professor Threcar announced. "You will drink it and it will help keep your powers under control. When I say that, I mean that it will help you with the soakings, the icy air, the fingernail pain, et cetera. From now on, before class officially starts, you will each drink one cupful."

We murmured to each other in excitement.

She passed out blue cups with liquid bubbling in them. The temperature around the cup was icy cold, and a pretty gross smell arose from the contents.

"Now, drink."

We all obeyed. I took a sip of my potion. It was cool, sliding down my throat in an icy gulp. It felt refreshing, but the taste was disgusting.

"Drink it all."

It was more than disgusting, but we knew we had to drink it. So I gulped it down while I tried not to taste the gross stuff in it. There was a tinge of something a little tasty—maybe it was the watermelon flavor, but even that seemed to have been affected by the rest of the repulsive stuff.

When I had it down, I walked up to Professor Threcar. "What is *in* that?" I asked.

She grinned. "Nicange, a little Visidia and Ditunium, and Liitupler."

"What?" I asked. It sounded like she was speaking gibberish or something!

She smiled again, the skin around her eyes crinkling. "A Nicange is like a cross between an orange and a pineapple, an orange spiky ball that is rather disgusting. A Visidia is rather like a banana mixed with a plum; a very expensive, valuable fruit grown only in the Sky Garden." *The what?* "A Ditunium is a star-shaped brown-and-white-watermelon. These grow in the Sky Garden, too. And a Liitupler is a hybrid between lettuce and a hot pepper, sweet at first, with a bitter aftertaste."

"I didn't know there were so many magical fruits."

"Oh, that's only the beginning."

Great. This was going to be so much fun, memorizing all of the fruits and veggies. Yay! So *not*!

After we had drunk the potion, Professor Threcar talked some more about the ingredients. It was interesting, but it was going to take a *lot* of memorizing.

We had a lot of spare time today. Classes were over by 3:00, so from 3:00 until 6:00, we just lounged around. It was not very entertaining. After watching TV for an hour, I decided to take a broom ride, so I flew around Dream Ring and just thought. Then I practiced doing easy spells with Victoria. By six, I was going out of my mind. I had studied for all upcoming pop quizzes, tests, exams, or possible subjects of discussion.

At 6:00, I started to get ready. I got into a comfy outfit, just sweatpants and a long-sleeved T-shirt. Then I put on my long, cashmere, midnight blue robes (they're considered very dressy in the witch and wizard society, and you couldn't see my sweatpants anyway), and some flip-flops. I put my hair in one long braid, and put in some fake-diamond earrings that looked real. Victoria and I left by 6:30, so that we could take the long way to the main hall on our brooms.

When we got there, we were seated at our normal places. They gave us seats next to our friends, which was totally cool, and each place had only a headset and our name card.

"Attention, students!" Licklici said. The entire school was here tonight, and the hall was packed. The only people on the entire planet who weren't here were the teachers. Apparently, they already had the scoop, so they didn't attend. Tonight Licklici was wearing purple satin robes and white, four-inch high heels. Her hair was curled in ringlets and pulled back in a barrette. Her eyes sparkled with excitement, and her cheeks were flushed with happiness. "My announcement concerns all students here at Dream Ring. Recently we recruited two new staff members, Professors Jolty and Treeny. They will be teaching your new classes, Charms and Gardening."

She paused for dramatic effect, and we looked at each other with silent groans.

"In Charms, you will learn, well, how to execute charms. And in Gardening, you will learn about the magical fruits and vegetables, and get to visit and care for the… Sky Garden. These classes will be just like your other classes, meeting on campus. You will get directions on your pass.

"One more announcement. This second half of the second semester, you will have each class every day. Class periods will be less than an hour each, and you will get one study break.

"Are there any questions?"

One student shouted out, "Yeah. Why?"

"Because the staff at Dream Ring believes that if a class is taken every day, students retain more information. And during this last part of the year you will need to learn a lot of things. Are there any more questions?"

There weren't, so we ordered our food, and the feast began.

The feast was always fun, and tonight was even more exciting. The food that we had learned to cook in our dorms was okay, but it wasn't amazing. Here in the hall, though, when you could imagine what you wanted, everything was cooked *exactly* how you wanted. I wished for a homemade steak-and-cheese quesadilla, a fruit salad, and a piece of chocolate-chocolate-chocolate cake. It all tasted delicious, so I ate the wonderful food and then wished for leftovers in a bag. Yum.

When the feast was over, we filed out of the main hall, headed back to our dorms, and relaxed for the rest of the night.

Chapter Twenty Five

"Ava. It's time to get up. We have Charms in ten."

I was definitely awake now. "Ten, as in ten *minutes*?"

Victoria nodded. "Yep!"

I sprang out of bed, pausing once to look at the clock. I groaned. I definitely was not enjoying this whole "every class, every day," thing.

By the time I looked half presentable I was ten minutes late for our first class. Luckily, Professor Jolty was also a little slow in the mornings, so class was just getting started.

Professor Jolty was very old-looking, tall and skinny. He had deep sunken bags under his eyes, like he hadn't slept in months. His voice was deep and gravelly, and his hair was a dull gray, short, and it stuck up in the back. He wore emerald robes that covered his toes, so I couldn't tell whether he had shoes on.

"I am Professor Jolty. You are here for Charms. This class is hard, so study very diligently." He paused to have a very long coughing fit. "A charm has been put on me." He grinned at us, and started to laugh, a startling, rattling laugh that sent shivers down my spine. Midway through his laughing fit, his voice broke and he started to cough again. We just stared at him until he stopped his fit and began to talk again. "Arthkapoli, which is an 'old people' charm." Then he laughed again, but this time he was able to stop normally and speak again.

Was this dude joking? I couldn't tell. He certainly looked old, but maybe it *was* the effect of a charm.

"No, seriously!" he insisted, and for a second I could hear a young voice come out of the old man.

"You are here to learn charms. I will be kind to you if you are kind to me. The charm that is making me old and sick is supposed to wear off a week from now. So please bear with"— a coughing fit—"me while I deal with this. An old enemy of mine gave it to me. I guess he thought it would be funny."

He kept on talking, and halfway through the period I zoned out. I began to daydream…

"OLLIOPHUS!!" I suddenly heard my ancient-who-wasn't-ancient teacher shout. I snapped out of my daydream and looked at him. His wand was pointed at Ella, and her eyes were lit up with fright. This man was definitely a little cuckoo, but it was also rather exciting to see what he would do to my "friend."

Suddenly I saw a change in Ella. She started to shrink down, and where her nose would have been, a beak appeared. Her toes underneath her robes became talons, and I think I heard a squawk of protest.

I blinked, and when I looked at Ella again, *she* wasn't there. She was an honest-to-God *hawk*. I'm not kidding. It's true—he had turned her into a *hawk*.

"What did you do to her?" Kathryn screeched at Professor Jolty.

"That was a simple charm. I can reverse it easily," he replied. And he did, thankfully. The only thing different about her afterwards was that feathers occasionally fell out of her clothes and hair, and every so often her laugh sounded a little like a bird chirping.

Okay, there was no way that I was ever going to daydream in this class again!

The rest of the class was pretty boring. I mean, we went over the basics of doing charms, and the hazards, and how you should never do a charm if you don't know the reverse, *blah blah blah*.

But since Professor Jolty did that spazzy charm to Ella, I had new respect for the old-who-wasn't-old man.

⋰⋰❋⋱⋱

We filed into the greenhouse, everybody wondering what this new class would be like.

At the front of the greenhouse stood a short, squat man. He was wearing green gloves and brown robes, a complete earth man. He had a goatee, a unibrow, and pig-like squinty eyes. His hair was buzzed close to his head.

"Hello!" he announced, then sniffed four times. "You must be Yurnia freshmen. I am Professor... TREENY!" he sang.

We nodded.

"You are... YURNIAN... FIRST... YEARS!!" he sang in a loud, hearty voice, his arms raised in the air. Then he sniffed.

"You are here for my tremendous Gardening class," he said, sniffing thoughtfully. "I should probably begin class," he said to himself, then sniffed again loudly.

"We will be learning the magical fruits and vegetables." *Sniff, sniff.* "The people who get all A's in Gardening for the second semester will take an exclusive field trip to the Sky Garden." *(Sniff, sniff, stroke the goatee.)*

"Today we will start by watering all of the plants in the greenhouse with magical Nicange juice. It helps the plants grow fully magical. I assume that Professor Threcar told you what a Nicange is when you first drank the Power-Helping potion. Right?" *Sniff, sniff, sniff.*

He handed us each a watering can filled halfway with a yellow-orange juice that smelled—bad. It was steaming a little bit. I held it at arm's length and wandered over to a couple of plants. Some were growing right before my eyes, some were snapping at me with teeth, others were looking at me with actual eyes.

Creepy, I thought. I finally found a plant that looked pretty normal, except for the fact that it was bright blue with yellow stripes. I could handle vivid colors, just not, like, humanly-alive plants.

I sprinkled some of the yellow-orange juice on it and the plant shot up about four inches. I watered the other plants, and by the time I had finished with three, class was almost over.

"Goodbye... YURNIAN... FIRST... YEARS!" Professor Treeny sang spontaneously. Then he sniffed quite a few times. "GO-ODBYE!"

This dude was hilarious, and maybe a little too jolly, but I thought I could deal with him. And the Sky Garden could be really fun.

Chapter Twenty Six

The next day Licklici called us downstairs to the main hall to announce that Mr. Minaga and Professor Gophersmocker would be helping us with more spells in defense.

"Why not Professor Threcar?" I asked. Mr. Minaga was *not* my favorite professor at all. What if he tried to harm one of us? We could all be in danger.

Professor Gophersmocker jumped right in. "Her great-great-grandmother is sick, and she had to go to Saturn to, um, say goodbye to her. She will probably be back in two weeks. For that time, Licklici will be your teacher for Potions and Powers. But today's lesson in spell-fights will be with me and Mr. Minaga. Let's give him a warm welcome," he said.

Students who didn't know his true identity clapped enthusiastically. I lazily put my hands together about three times before silently booing my teacher. I knew it was disrespectful, but I also knew he was evil, so I figured that got me a free pass.

"Now, for today's spell, we are going to learn how to put people to sleep—only for a minute, of course."

Mr. Minaga said, "Gophersmocker, I'll take it from here."

Put people to sleep? No way. That sounded like a really good chance for Mr. Minaga to hand us over to his best friend, the "Master" (not!) Widdidorm.

"Now, to put someone to sleep, like Professor Gophersmocker said, briefly, hold your wand over the person's head and say 'slumber-OSA.' The person will fall asleep immediately. When you say 'slumber-OSA,' immediately a charm will be put on all objects surrounding the person that could harm him or her so he or she is safe to just fall down. Now, there is a way this spell can go wrong. If you say 'slumber-iumptia,' the person will be put in a coma. I know I shouldn't tell you this, but I want to warn you in case someone tries to do this to you. It won't happen, but just in case. There's a spell like that to kill a person, too, but there's no way I would give you that one." He smiled mischievously, and I knew he knew it and was waiting to try it out on someone. "Now, students, seriously. Try this on your friends, and ka-boom! Well, more like zzzz's.

"If you know that someone is trying the coma or death spell on you, shout 'defend-IFFERUS!' This will build a shield around you for as long as you can keep your focus on your wand and the spell. Once this force-field ends, you can't put another one on yourself for ten minutes, so I would escape in the interim or use another spell when this wears down.

"Now, we're going to try this. I only want to hear 'slumber-OSA.' Use of the coma spell will result in suspension and other proceedings. When I give the 'go,' one partner can say 'slumber-OSA' and the other can do the defensive charm, which is, again, defend-IFFERUS. Right now I only want you to try the 'slumber-OSA,' though. All right, begin!"

I paired up with Victoria and got ready to do the spell. "You can go first," I told her.

She held the wand positioned over my head, and I waited to just fall over. She squinched her eyes shut and said softly "slumberosa" in a frightened voice. Nothing happened. I was still awake, and Victoria still had her eyes shut and a frown on her face.

"Vic," I said. "I think that you're supposed to say it with a lot of force and a big accent on the 'OSA.' Try it again."

This time she was cool and confident. A big smile on her face, she held the wand over my head and said loudly, "SLUMBER-OSA!" All of a sudden a wave of drowsiness spread through me. I felt warm and cozy. And then I hit the floor with a dull *thud*. Surprisingly, I wasn't hurt at all.

I slept like a baby for all of two minutes. Then I woke with a start to see Victoria looking at me with a face full of concern. "I'm awake. I'm good," I told her.

She smiled in relief and said, "Now it's your turn."

I held my wand over her head and said the magic words. She collapsed just as I had, sleeping for a minute-and-a-half before she woke up.

"Next we're going to practice using the force-field. I'll have two students come up here and demonstrate with me so that we can show everyone how to do it. How about... Zach and... Ava Popolis. Come on up, lady and gentleman. Zach, you can go first. Mr. Minaga, let's do it."

Mr. Minaga stepped forward on the raised platform and Zach stood ready. Fortunately I had faith in Zach; he was a pretty good wizard.

"SLUMBER-*OSA*!" Mr. Minaga shouted loud and clear. At the same moment, Zach said timidly, "Defend-IFFERUS," and a small, clear bubble started to form around him. Slowly it began to gain color until a solid white shape protected him. Once Mr. Minaga finished his spell, the force-field disappeared.

"Great job, Zach!" to which Zach responded by promptly fainting on the floor for all of the first-years to see.

"Well," Professor Gophersmocker said, glancing at Zach, who was passed out on the floor, "this *is* some tough magic. Maybe we should have saved this for second years..." He sighed.

"Ava, you're up. Count to five, then let the force-field drop, so we don't have a repeat of Zach," Professor Gophersmocker said, as Nurse Norah propped the unconscious Zach into a wheelchair and wheeled him away.

Shaking nervously, I stepped onto the raised platform. Mr. Minaga stepped forward and I started feeling sleepy again. Fighting that, I got my wand ready.

I waited for him to shout the spell for the whole world to hear, but all I heard was a muttered spell, one that sounded like 'slumber-iumptia.' I jumped when I heard the suffix and immediately shouted clearly, "Defend-IFFERUS!" Fortunately my spell took effect quickly, and a very solid white shield encircled me so that nothing could penetrate. I held this for a full minute in case Mr. Minaga was still muttering curses above me. By then the magic had knocked me out; but I knew that it wouldn't be eternal—somehow I had managed to save myself.

I fell to the floor as I fainted. I heard frantic voices around me and then the wheels of a stretcher magically propelling themselves toward me. Don't ask how I knew all of this when I was knocked out, I have no clue. Somehow I just did.

Chapter Twenty Seven

I woke up in the middle of the night in an uncomfortable bed. (I guess I got better treatment when I broke my wrist; that bed was much more comfortable.) I couldn't remember where I was or why I was here.

Suddenly the lights flickered on. Standing in front of me was Nurse Norah, her face creased and worried. When she saw that I was awake, she cried out in joy. "You're alive! Ava, you're here! You're on Neptune! Not in Heaven, Neptune! Amber! *Come in here!*"

My guard from Yurnia appeared in the doorway. Her face lit up when she saw my eyes were open and my heart was pumping blood, which wasn't exactly a shock to me. Then Nurse Norah quickly ran back into the medicine room and poured out a blue cup full of steaming liquid that smelled foul. Unfortunately I knew what it was: my disgusting Power-Helping potion.

"This is the only thing that you can take right now to help you recover from your, uh, incident. Now, Ava, I don't want to frighten you, but, um, do you remember what happened last night?"

Memories came back. "Uh, yeah," I said. "We were going to do the same thing that Zach did, but when Mr. Minaga said the spell he said 'slumber-iumptia,' so I quickly did a force-field. I held the force-field for as long as I could in case Mr. Minaga was still trying to injure me. The effort of holding such hard magic knocked me out."

"The effort of holding such hard magic knocked you out?"

"Yes, ma'am."

She asked the question again.

"Nurse?"

"Yes?" The distracted look left her eyes, and she turned her full attention on me.

"Why do you keep repeating yourself?"

"Well, I guess because I'm fairly sure that Minaga was close to killing you. Maybe you were knocked out for so long because he half-killed you with the strength of the coma spell, almost petrified you, but not quite. You know what I mean?"

I must have been wearing my thinking face, because she looked frightened. "Are you okay? Did I scare you too much?" she asked worriedly.

"No, no. I'm good. I have to say I disagree. I mean, I think it was just the magic thing. Is Mr. Minaga fired?"

"No. He is on probation, and his records are being inspected to see if he is safe to continue as a teacher at Dream Ring."

"Good. He should be fired."

"Ava! You do not talk so disrespectfully about a teacher!"

"But he *tried* to *kill* me!" I told her.

She just pursed her lips and walked away.

I couldn't believe it! I mean, I was the one that it happened to, but she didn't believe me! I *knew* that Mr. Minaga was bad. He was evil! But nobody would listen.

Nurse Norah said that I had to stay in bed for three days. Three *days*! So I read, I studied, I was a good girl. But eventually, I got antsy. Really antsy.

"Hey Victoria," I whispered on my little mobile phone that was in my pocket. "Come on up. I need to talk to you."

"I don't know about this," she said, unconvinced.

"C'mon. I'm dying up here. I have to stay for another day."

"Okay. I'll be up in ten minutes. I have to braid Kathryn's hair first and then eat."

"Random, but okay."

"See ya in a few."

A few minutes later Victoria entered my hospital room. The place was a too-cheerful pink, with roses everywhere, and on top of that the bed was pretty uncomfortable. It wasn't the best place to stay on Neptune.

"How are you?" Victoria asked.

"Hanging in there. I feel back to normal now, but I still have another day."

"That stinks." She squeezed my hand in best-friend solidarity.

"I know, right?"

She nodded. "Okay, so how did it feel when you got knocked out after holding the force-field too long?"

"What are you, a reporter? Already starting in with the questions." I grinned, and then said, "Well, I felt really tired, drained. I just kind of fell down," I started. "Wait. What did Minaga do after I fainted?"

"Well, after he said the spell, he ran off really quick. His face was white, and he looked really scared because he realized that Licklici was watching."

"Wow. Then what happened?" I asked.

"Um, well, Licklici made some quick phone calls, and her face was red, and then pale. She immediately called her husband, Frank, down for some backup, and he brought security."

"Oh, my," I said.

"How did you feel when you woke up in the hospital room?"

"I felt really, really tired. I tried doing a spell, but I couldn't and that made me feel really exhausted."

"Hmm. What did Nurse Norah say?" Victoria asked.

"She said she thinks I was knocked out for so long because Minaga was close to actually killing me."

"Is that true?" Victoria's fists clenched in anticipated stress and her face took on a pained expression.

"I don't *think* so."

"Well, that's good." Victoria's facial expression relaxed and she quit gripping the plastic chair she was sitting in.

"Well, you gotta help me get outta here. It's horrible just sitting in bed all day. The only way that I can get out of bed is to go to the bathroom. I can't even shower!" I exclaimed, hoping that my dramatic speech would push her over the edge and motivate her to get me out.

"What can I do?"

"You can convince Nurse Norah that I'm fine," I said sweetly, giving her a huge smile.

"I can try," she said, smiling.

"Thank you!" I squealed.

"Keep it down in there!" Nurse Norah hollered through the door.

I waited for, like, ten minutes before Victoria came back in. "Sorry," she said sadly, giving me a sympathetic look. "I tried. I really did."

"Thank you for trying," I said. "Visit me."

"I will. Hey, you get to come back to Yurnia tomorrow. And today you can write a letter to your mom or something."

Dear Mom,

So Minaga tried to kill me!!

I know, like, a million things are racing through your head right now, Mom. "What happened?" "Are you okay?"

We were showing the rest of the first-years how to do a "Put to Sleep" charm and I was supposed to do a "Defending" charm. But, he put a "Coma" charm on me, and fortunately, I blocked it before it was fatal, but I held the force-field as long as I could, in case he was still trying to kill me, or put me in a coma or whatever. He wasn't, and I knocked myself out with the effort of the defensive charm.

Nurse Norah has kept me in the hospital wing for three whole days while I recover! Frankly, I was all better by the second day and now I'm just sitting in torture. Literally. The bed is so uncomfortable!

Please write a letter of recommendation to Licklici telling her that Minaga needs to be fired.

Please don't be too scared. I'm fine. I mean, I was really tired and drained the first day I was awake, but I'm better now. Victoria tried to get me out of the infirmary earlier, but to no avail.

Love ya!

Ava

Dear Ava,

He what?!?!?! I can't believe that a teacher would do something like that! But then again, Mr. Minaga isn't really your average teacher. Are you sure you're okay? Maybe I'd better come up to check on you.

It really worries me, Ava. We can't have teachers like this at Dream Ring. Are you really okay? This worries me, Ava. It really does.

I'll be coming to check on you the weekend of April 26th, in three weeks. Please tell Licklici of my plans. She never was really happy about unexpected visitors.

Try to stay safe.

Mom

Oh no. This wasn't good. I had to act. Fast!

Dear Mom,

No, it is NOT a good idea for you to come here to protest against Minaga. It would make things worse. Besides, he's already on probation and being investigated! I'm serious. Don't come!

Please don't!

I am fine. I'm serious. I am OKAY. Nurse Norah said that I might even be able to leave a bit earlier than predicted.

(Okay. That was a lie, but it was necessary in order to keep Mom OFF Neptune. She couldn't do that to me—it would make everything worse! She just couldn't.)

Please send me a return letter so that I know that you're not coming, okay? Please don't. I'm telling you, it would make Minaga madder.

~A

Dear Ava,

I have seen your reason. I know that my visiting would make MISTER Minaga (he is NOT just 'Minaga'; remember your manners—it's Mr. Minaga to you) more angry. It might provoke him to do something worse, and considering my history with him, it could do some big damage.

Thank you for convincing me. I hope to hear from you soon.

Love, Mom

p.s. Don't go looking for trouble. I MEAN IT!

Phew! She wasn't coming. What a relief! It would've been bad if she had come. Minaga—sorry, *MR*. Minaga—could try again, and, to state the obvious, that would be bad. Very bad.

Plus, it would be embarrassing. Unfortunately, my mother can be that way.

The stress-fest with my mother led me to believe that a nap was in order for my recovery and relief of parental issues. After thinking it over for three seconds, I snuggled deep into the covers and drifted off.

Chapter Twenty Eight

Victoria and I hurried out of Charms and ran to Potions. We were having more end-of-semester exams today and could *not* afford to be late. As (sort of) smart as I am, I still needed all the time for the exam that I could get.

In Potions we drew cards with the names of Potions on them and directions on how to make them. Then we had the rest of class to efficiently make the potion. At the end of class Professor Threcar tested the potions to see if they worked.

I drew the Invisibility Potion. Since one of my powers was Potions, I knew it almost by heart. I took about two looks at the recipe card, and whipped it up. I turned in my potion with about twenty minutes to spare, and Professor Threcar tested it. It worked, and I saw her mark an 'A' on my paper. Yes! Two down, seven to go. This was the second day of exams.

We got one day of rest while the tests were scored. Some of them were hands-on, like Potions. Others were tests with multiple-choice questions.

Even though the day of rest was well-earned, it wasn't much fun. Everyone in Yurnia was antsy and quiet. We sat in the living room all day watching TV, reading, and talking. Eventually I got so bored that I took a broom ride. I knew that it was against the rules to go off campus and off Neptune, but I rode out of the atmosphere and took a ride on Neptune's rings. Riding on the giant frozen slides cleared my head, and I stopped worrying about tests and exams.

As I was completing my first orbit of the planet, about an hour-and-a-half later (I had used my Weather power to make my bottom ice-proof), I saw someone ahead of me. I slid a little closer, then halted myself by dragging my fingernails into the ice. I don't know how that stopped my entire body weight plus broom, but it did.

I peered very closely at the person about one hundred feet away. He was muttering to a faint ghost that looked suspiciously like how Widdidorm had appeared in my dream.

Then it hit me. Mr. Minaga was meeting Widdidorm one hundred feet away from me on the rings of Neptune.

I froze, almost literally. I wished I had the Invisibility Potion, but unfortunately I was too far away to use my magic to bring it to me. I wasn't *that* good yet.

I hadn't moved since I realized Mr. Minaga was so close to me and, slowly, my worst nightmare turned to reality: he started walking towards me.

My feet refused to move. The only part that did something *smart* was my hand. It immediately grabbed my wand out of my robe pocket and held it, ready to defend or blind or *anything*. I was desperate.

I saw Minaga's eyes narrow as he recognized me. I started to step forward, but I tripped and fell flat on my butt. Along with the pain, the fall held me motionless long enough for Mr. Minaga to reach my side.

"*You* again," he sneered, his greasy hair brushing my shoulder as he paced beside me. "I almost killed you."

"Almost."

"If I were you, I would be quiet, girl."

I was in agreement there. I had been so stupid to make such a sassy remark.

"I just want you to know that when my Master says I can, then I *will* kill you."

I just nodded meekly. He was now bent over, about seven inches from my face, and his hand grasped his wand like a gun.

This wasn't looking good for me.

"But unfortunately," he continued sadly, "Master wants me to spare you for the time being. He wants to kill you *himself*. I would've liked to do the honors, but I must obey."

I nodded again.

"So. I'm giving you a warning, *girl*," he sneered in my face, spit flying at my cheeks, chin, forehead, and nose. "You better be *careful*. You're a smart one, girl." (*What's with the "girl" thing?* some part of my mind wondered). "You just missed my spell. I almost had you. But unfortunately, you slipped away, and now I'm the bad guy."

I didn't nod here. It would look like I agreed with him that he's the bad guy, and that wouldn't look good. I mean, I did agree, but this wasn't the time to say that.

"So you need to watch your back, because my Master is planning revenge for your mother's mistake."

Then he disappeared with a flick of his wand, and I was stuck sitting on Neptune's rings with my broom in one hand and my wand in the other.

My mother's *MISTAKE!? WHAT!?*

She was going to hear from me.

❦

The next day we received our report cards:

DREAM RING, NEPTUNE
Second Semester Report Card
Student: Ava Popolis

(*"NT"=not taken*)

Math (*Professor Addsubmerd*): A-

Science *(Professor Lorn):* A-

Literature *(Professor Bird):* B+

Powers Against Evil Witchcraft *(Professor Gophersmocker):* C-

Flying *(Mrs. Gophersmocker):* A+

Musical Magic Against Evil *(Mr. Minaga):* NT

Medication Using Magic: NT

Stargazing *(Professor Eleema):* A+

Fortune Telling *(Madam Tralah):* B+

Woodworking: NT

Wishful Thinking: NT

Technology with Magic: NT

Charms *(Professor Jolty):* A

Potions *(Professor Threcar):* A+

Powers *(Professor Threcar):* A

Gardening *(Professor Treeny):* A

COMMENTS:

(Flying) *Ava has done exceptionally well for her first year. I hope that she will try out for our sport next year.*

(Math) *I am very proud of how Ava brought her grade up.*

(Powers Against Evil Witchcraft) *As Ava has had a couple brushes with potentially evil wizards, I feel that she should have studied more. It was very disappointing when she got a below average grade on her final exam.*

(Fortune Telling) *Ava pays attention consistently. It is an honor to have her as a student.*

Headmistress Signature: _____

Parent Signature: _____

Student Signature: _____

Tardy: 7 times

Absent: 2 times

I was pretty excited about my report card. For the most part, I did pretty well. I was happy that I had received good grades. The hard part would be telling Mom about my Powers Against Evil Witchcraft grade. She would probably become hysterical about that, on top of my many brushes with Mr. Minaga this year. I could just picture her: she would wear black robes and her fingernails would be positively black. She would cry when she saw the grade, and then we would have a long "talk," which meant an hour's lecture about how I needed to study more. I would pretend to be sorry and then leave. It was pretty much right on schedule.

The parents were scheduled to come on May 16th, a week after we got our report cards. We were allowed out of school early so that we could go home at about the same time as most normal kids. Ha! We are *so* not normal kids!

To prepare for the closing of Dream Ring for the summer, Licklici made us clean the dorm until it shone so bright that she joked that our parents would need sunglasses. Licklici was in a good mood now that school was over. Now we had just free time, cleaning out our dorms and packing for the journey home.

And of course, there was also the Sky Garden field trip. On our last class, Professor Treeny announced that only ten people would be going on the exclusive field trip. I was shocked. I mean, Gardening had been really easy for me! But I guess a lot of people totally bombed the final exam, which brought their grades down a lot.

So Victoria, Kathryn, Ella, Josh, Jacob, Isaac, Tanya, Luke, Gabriella, and I would go on the trip. It would be really fun. I heard that last year one kid was bitten by the dragon who guards the entrance. That would be... um, eventful!

⚜

Strangely, I hadn't had any more visits from Mr. Minaga or Widdidorm. Minaga hadn't been making me sleepy, either! But I suspected something. I mean, Minaga had warned me and I knew that he was biding his time. They were, in fact, in for the kill.

Only four more days until Mom came—today was May 12th. But first, we were going on the Sky Garden field trip. We would leave tomorrow for two days. I was super excited.

We had a specific list of what we were supposed to bring:

1 Pair of magically-protected leather gloves

1 Cauldron

Gardening notebook and textbook

2 Watering cans, *one immune to rust (magically-treated—see Professor Treeny), one regular.*

1 Shovel

3 Sets of robes that can get dirty

Wand

Personal products for 2 nights

A signed permission slip from your parents allowing you to go on this field trip.

Chapter Twenty Nine

"Get *up*, girls!" Professor Threcar was in the Yurnia girls' dorm to wake us up bright and early. Let me rephrase that: dark and early. On Neptune, we sometimes get a few hours of bright, Earth-like sunlight, and that's almost always smack-dab in the middle of the day. The rest of the time there's sunlight, but it's dim, like twilight all day, if you know what I mean.

I groaned loudly. Professor Threcar walked over to my bed and pulled off my covers, revealing my blue tank top and black shorts underneath all the blankets. My hair was a mess, and I was groggy. I pulled up my blankets underneath my chin; I mean, it was VERY cold when you have short clothes on and you're on Neptune.

"Ava, it's time to get up," Professor Threcar gently reminded me. I groaned again. "We're going to the Sky Garden. That's a once-in-a-lifetime deal. And you need to get dressed too. You can't fly on Neptune like that without freezing."

"I know. But it's 4:15 in the morning!"

"Yes. And we should be out of here in less than 15 minutes."

Another groan. Thankfully, Professor Threcar left, and I was allowed to moan as much as I wanted without feeling like I was being disrespectful.

But the idea of missing the Sky Garden was not good either. So I rolled out of bed and slipped on more appropriate clothes: robes, sweatpants, and a long-sleeved T-shirt. Then I slipped on my pointed witch hat the professor wanted me to wear over my messy ponytail. I giggled at my reflection: I looked ridiculous! Hopefully this field trip would be worth the fashion sacrifice!

We put our luggage in the invisible cellar below our brooms. When everyone was gathered in the yard outside the main hall, we mounted our brooms.

"Now, class," Professor Treeny began, sniffing quite violently. "You are here for my... TREMENDOUS... SKY GARDEN... FIELD TRIP!" He burst spontaneously into a loud song with almost no melody. Then, of course, he sniffed and stroked his goatee. His unibrow seemed almost bushier than usual, if that's even possible.

Professor Threcar tapped his shoulder and whispered something in his ear, probably to hurry up.

"You need to follow"—(*sniff, sniff*)—"me until I find the Sky Garden cloud. I need"—(*stroke the goatee*)—"absolute silence in order to find the cloud."

We nodded, and a couple of kids fake-sniffed in mock of Professor Treeny, who must have an eternal cold or obsessive compulsive disorder or something.

"Great. Now"—*sniff*—"we must be on our way." He set off at a brisk pace.

We followed him.

And followed him.

And followed him some more.

I honestly thought that we had flown around Neptune about six times. I felt like I kept seeing the same landmarks over and over and over. It seemed like hours until we finally arrived at the cloud.

Finally we slowed down. Professor Treeny was looking up at an elongated cloud shaped like a banana. "This... IS... IT!" he sang loudly and triumphantly. "Ladies and gentlemen, madames and messieurs. I give you... the SKY GARDEN!" He waved his hands at the banana-shaped cloud.

"Now, as I was saying." He took out his wand, sniffed a couple of times, then muttered a spell. He got off his broom in mid-air and walked over to us ten first-years. *In mid-air.*

"I wanna learn *that* spell!" I exclaimed under my breath.

"Quiet, Popolis," Professor Treeny said firmly. "Now, as I was saying." *Sniff, sniff.*

I was feeling spicy, and I said, "You already said that."

"Popolis! Do not talk back."

"Sorry."

"Yes." *Sniff.* "As I was saying"—*stroke the goatee*—"we will land on that banana-shaped cloud, yep, there it is."—*Sniff.*—"And then from there we will transport to the Sky Garden. There is only one banana-shaped cloud in all of Neptune"—*stroke the goatee*—"and that's where the Sky Garden always is. Professor Threcar, anything to add?"

"Yes, thank you. You see, the Sky Garden has only been around for about nine years. So your parents have never had the privilege of being on this field trip. Now Professor Treeny takes students on these field trips, but only first-years, so this will likely be the only time in your life to go up here. Unless of course, the rules change, because some of these plants are important in second-year potions. I may just have to change the rules." She smiled mischievously at us. We smiled back.

"One more thing. Once we get there, most beings you'll see are pixies. They manage the Sky Garden, care for it, and make sure that everything is growing on track.

"But you *might* see two giants. You probably *won't* see them, but you might if you're lucky. They are the caretakers of the dragons that guard the entrances. Don't insult them—they may be giant, but they are very soft-hearted and will likely maim you for a mean remark. If you want to be their friend, you should just be silent.

"Does everyone remember what a pixie is?"

"Like Tinker Bell?" Ella asked.

"Sort of. They are small humans with wings. Their dust is magical and powerful, very rare. If a pixie offers you some pixie dust, never decline. It is very, very valuable.

"They also have a great understanding of all plants, magical and non-magical." *What would a pixie look like?* I wondered. *What would all of this look like?!*

"Now. We are going to fly up on the cloud, and store our brooms there. I will perform a spell over all of us, and I will need you all to repeat the phrase, 'Papa-Tar, Papa-Tar,' over and over. This will help me complete the spell without too much wear and tear on my magical abilities. Professor Treeny will also be helping us." Professor Treeny puffed up his chest at this.

"Ready? Here we go."

We flew on our brooms the short distance to the banana-shaped cloud that would get us to the Sky Garden. The cloud was the strangest thing that I've ever stood on, and that means a lot, as I've been on many different surfaces lately—for example, Neptune, Neptune's *rings*, a floating space station. You could see for miles beneath you, as it was almost transparent. As usual, Neptune looked amazingly beautiful, and I gasped at the view of the mountains and ocean. The actual cloud looked like thin, wispy cotton balls, but more resilient. You could jump up and down, and it would bounce with your motion, like a trampoline. I know, because I tried it.

Which earned me another "Popolis!"

I quit right then, because I sure didn't want a detention at the end of school year.

We stored our brooms on the end of the cloud and then moved into the middle, the thickest part.

I clutched my wand in the right pocket of my robes and focused on the gibberish words that I was supposed to say to help us appear at the Sky Garden.

"Go!" Professor Threcar said, taking her wand out and muttering a complicated spell. We all said "Papa-Tar, Papa-Tar, Papa-Tar, Papa-Tar," over and over again. I thought we sounded like idiots, but it must have worked because a minute later the atmosphere around me started spinning. The cloud vanished, and suddenly we were facing a great golden and marble gate. Two gargantuan dragons, black and orange and red, breathed fire while guarding the gates. It's a miracle that the marble and gold didn't melt because the air felt, like, four thousand degrees.

We were about one hundred feet from the dragons and I was sweating buckets already, probably the first time I'd done so naturally since coming to Neptune. Professor Threcar approached one of the dragons and touched a scale on its gigantic shoulder. I was afraid the dragon would set her on fire or totally burn her, but it didn't. Once she touched the scale, the dragon stopped flaming and curled up like a huge cat next to her. Then it snorted and started thrashing around, and Professor Threcar pulled something that looked suspiciously like a Slim Jim beef jerky stick out of her bag. She fed it to the dragon and he stopped spazzing out. After she had done the same to the other dragon, she walked up to the gates and slid a card into a golden pocket. The gates opened and she walked through.

Professor Threcar beckoned to Professor Treeny and the rest of us to follow her through the gates. Professor Treeny hadn't helped at all—he had just stood there sniffing and stroking his goatee. Typical.

Once we entered the gates, we were standing in a room called "Before-Garden," with plain gray walls and hard plastic chairs. It was drab, not at all what I had expected the Sky Garden to be.

"Now, class," Professor Threcar said, "I'll explain what you will see when you enter the Sky Garden, and what happened back there at the gates.

"You saw me touch the dragons' shoulder scales, right? Well, that lets them know that I'm not going to harm them, so they calm down."

"But the dragon snorted and went berserk," Victoria commented. "That's not what I call calm."

"Yes. I'm getting there. Their dragon DNA gets the better—"

"Professor?"

"Yes, Isaac?"

"Dragons have DNA?"

"Don't ask stupid questions. Of *course* they do. And please don't interrupt unless it is an emergency or you have a relatively intelligent question, okay?"

"Got it."

Professor Threcar got that kind of respect. Everybody liked her so much that they were intent on behaving well in her company. Even boys like Isaac, a high-strung, silly type, would be calm and composed with her. Well, most of the time.

"As I was saying. Their DNA gets the better of them—" she shot a strict look at Isaac here—"and they have to go wild for a minute. If you know the correct food to offer, they will be perfectly content."

It was very hard here to not ask if that correct food was a Slim Jim.

"I fed the dragon a Slim Jim. It's not a certain brand or a certain kind; any kind of meat works. Once the dragons are calm, you approach the gate and insert your identification card. All witches and wizards receive one when they graduate from Dream Ring. Anyway, I inserted it into the slot.

"This is the long version: once the card is entered in, the card's number is transferred to a magical computer that the pixies maintain. The card shows them the entire history of your time at Dream Ring and here on Neptune, as well as any criminal record—on Earth or anywhere else. If they feel you're eligible, they let you in. In my case, they knew I was coming with you first-years. If I came on my own and without warning, the pixies would have some questions before they let me go inside.

"So the whole point of this lecture is to assure you that no dark wizard will enter the Garden. Some of these fruits and vegetable hybrids are very rare and valuable for important potions. But fortunately, the pixies are very much on top of things. So it won't happen."

I raised my hand. "Does Widdidorm know what makes dragons calm?" Professor Treeny gasped and put his hand to his heart when I said his name, then sniffed and stroked his goatee. The rest of the students, as they had heard of him but didn't know the nitty-gritty details, just stared.

"Good question. Actually, most people do know what calms a dragon. Fortunately, Widdidorm's card reveals a lot about him. The pixies would reject him and then let the dragons loose to kill him. If that was possible."

"Isn't it possible to kill Widdidorm? I mean, he is human, isn't he?"

Professor Threcar paled a little bit and I could see that she didn't want to answer my question. "We're getting a little off topic here."

She handed out a sheet that was several pages long and filled with information. "Now. I'm going to give you students a tour of the Garden, *and* you will meet some of my special pixie friends. This—" she held up the sheet—"is an outline of all the fruit and vegetable hybrids that grow here. We have every single magical food and potion ingredient here. We will only be touring the most rare and valuable hybrids in the Garden as it is too big for only two days."

"I have one more thing to add." Professor Treeny held up his hand and sniffed. "There are two rules." He stroked his goatee. "Number One is to not... touch... *anything*. Number Two"— I could tell he was leading up to a song—"is... HAVE... *FUN*!"

How do I know these things?

"Got it?"

"Yes, Professor."

"Good. Now, when we go in there it is going to be *amazing*. I have been up here many times and it still takes my breath away. And absolutely *no touching anything*. Do you guys understand the rules? And please stay about ten feet away from the nearest magical plant. I don't want to be held responsible for destroying anything or for affecting you!

"We'll observe here for two hours, and then have lunch at our hotel. Later, we'll come back for about an hour for a special feast the pixies are giving us. At midnight, we will harvest a plant and make a potion from it. Tomorrow we will tend the greenhouse, then make more potions and poke around a bit. Sound good?"

It sounded pretty darn good to me. These were really valuable plants, and we would get to harvest and tend and *everything*!

"Let's go, then!"

She opened the dull, gray door. I held my breath, it was so *beautiful*! The sky was perfect, the color of clearest blue that there is. The grass was perfectly cut, lush, and a rich green. And then the plants... they were incredible, and they were everywhere, spread out in neat rows or just growing wherever there was a spare patch of fertile, rich soil. About a million pixies tended a plant that was *black* and *green*. I'm not kidding!

One small pixie, only an inch or two tall, flitted around a big hose. When she snapped her fingers, the hose turned on and what looked like golden honey flowed out into a watering can! She clutched the watering can, which was quite small, too, and dragged it over to the black and green plant, which she proceeded to water. With *honey*!

The plants were all shapes and sizes, and all different colors. A large field of flowers bloomed near the entrance. They were all different colors, and they glowed with a certain shine that only pixies could produce. You honestly could not walk in that incredible field without crushing a flower, and as much as I wanted to be in the midst of the field, I held back because I didn't want to harm a single blossom.

There was a certain glow about this place, so perfect, almost what I pictured Heaven like. The air around the most valuable plants was swarming with pixies. The pixies had wings, of course, so they flew around, sometimes shrinking themselves so they could get closer to the plants. Sometimes, though, they enlarged until they were about three feet tall. It was quite fascinating to see a pixie change from a few inches to a few feet tall!

Professor Threcar's face was positively shining, and I saw her wipe away a tear or two. Professor Treeny looked a little less piggish than normal, and he actually stopped stroking his goatee long enough to shake hands with Professor Threcar's best pixie friend, Poppy.

Poppy was very small, with pitch-black hair the same color as Professor Threcar's. She wore a gold dress, tiny gold slippers, and one ring—that she wore as a bracelet. For most humans, her earrings would've been called studs, but on her they looked huge. (She was most definitely in her small form—only a few inches tall. She fluttered above us so that we could all hear her.)

"Hello, class," she said in a tinny voice. "What is your first impression of the Sky Garden?"

We all started to speak at once, but she shushed us. "Never mind. I can see it on your faces."

Poppy escorted us to a greenhouse, where we looked at the indoor plants. I thought it would be really boring with Professors Treeny and Threcar talking all the time, but it was actually really interesting. Poppy talked a lot too, which was cool, coming from a real employee of the Sky Garden. Some of the plants that we learned about were the Visidia, the Ditunium, the Urfmine, and the Tengurin. Poppy explained that there were lots more, but these were the most interesting. Surprisingly, those were the only plants that we learned about for the two hours we were at the greenhouse.

Professor Threcar and Poppy led us back to the gray room where Poppy had to say goodbye. "We'll be back after lunch, in about three hours," Professor Threcar assured her. "Goodbye!"

We returned to the gates and calmed the dragons again. "To go back to our destination, this time you will say, "Tar-Papa, Tar-Papa," Professor Threcar instructed. We spoke the words, and suddenly we were back on the banana-shaped cloud. Which, I experienced, was as bouncy as ever.

Professor Threcar announced, "We are going to descend to Neptune. After about five minutes' flight we will reach the Lone Hotel. Its name serves its purpose. The owners are only here once a year when students travel to the Sky Garden, although it's also open during harvesting season. Teams of harvesters travel from other planets to help us collect our special fruit and vegetable hybrids. We'll eat lunch at the hotel and store our luggage in our rooms. Then we'll fly back."

At the hotel we went immediately to the lunchroom, where we were served fried chicken, cucumber salad, macaroni and cheese, and milk. For dessert we had cheesecake. It was the first time I hadn't personally ordered my food on Neptune when eating with my teachers.

While we were eating, Professor Threcar paired us into roommates. "Victoria, Ava. Ella, Kathryn. Tanya, Gabriella. Josh, Luke. Jacob, Isaac." Victoria and I looked at each other and grinned. "Roomies!" we squealed. Even if it was just two days, it would be the first time that we would have time to ourselves since, like, August.

We stashed our stuff in the hotel, which was an exact mini-replica of a Holiday Inn that we stayed at in Colorado. It was kind of a disappointment, because I had hoped it might be special in some way.

We still had a few hours, so we just hung out in our rooms, chilling for the first time in several days. The rest felt good, but I was ready to get back to the Garden.

Chapter Thirty

After the break, we went back to the Sky Garden, where we learned more about rare fruits and vegetables and got to explore a little bit. Then we were invited into the pixies' dining hall. Candles floated about five feet above the long table that seated all of the tiny pixies and our twelve normal-size humans.

The head pixie, named Monique, snapped her fingers (quite loudly for such a small creature) and food appeared. A salad, a veggie burger, carrot sticks with Ranch dressing appeared, and we had chocolate mousse for dessert. (I'm still utterly confused about why we didn't have any exotic plants from the Sky Garden). The pixies must be vegetarian because we had no meat at the table. Everything was delicious except the veggie burger, which I've never really liked.

The feast disappeared the minute we declared ourselves full. Then a blue goblet, full of steaming liquid, appeared at each of our places. "Drink up!" Professor Threcar said. "You need your Power-Helping potion." Not that it would help much, I thought.

Professor Threcar said it kept us under control, but so far I had no proof. We groaned. We had thought that we wouldn't have to drink it on this field-trip/vacation!

"Yes, Mother," Isaac muttered ill-humoredly underneath his breath. I giggled softly.

While we were at the Sky Garden, we had a half hour to pick out postcards to send magically to our parents. Mine was a picture of the field of flowers. My note filled up the entire back.

Dear Mom,

Hello from the Sky Garden! I got an A in Gardening, so I got to go on this field trip with nine other students. It's so cool! I can't wait to tell you all about it, but we only have a couple of hours before we go to harvest a rare plant at midnight. So exciting!

I can't wait to see you! By the time you get this you will be almost ready to leave for Neptune for the end of semester. And then... I get to come home with you! I can't wait to be on Earth again. But surprisingly, I like Neptune a lot.

Love, Ava

p.s. Are we allowed to use our wands on Earth?

We waited in the main hall until 11:30. Then we followed Poppy and Monique and about a thousand other pixies outside. We would be harvesting the Urfmine. Only about twenty of these plants grew in the whole garden and tonight was the only night that anyone was allowed to harvest them. We would be using them in a potion at midnight because the vegetable can't be off the plant for very long before adding it to the potion.

I checked my watch as we gathered around the Urfmine: 11:48 P.M.

The Urfmine is a round blue-and-green plant that has milky kernels on the inside. It's a rare mix between rhubarb and corn. Weird, huh? I was dying to see the actual plant, but we couldn't see it at all; the Urfmine is enveloped in leaves that bite you if you try to harvest it prematurely. You have to chop the plant exactly at midnight and then you only have ninety-five seconds to add it to the potion. If you don't use the Urfmine right, it could kill you.

"Okay, class, listen up. Four vegetables grow to a stalk. So Isaac, Jacob, Ella, and Ava will pick at midnight. Then we will quickly hand the veggie to Luke, Josh, Tanya, Gabriella, Kathryn, and Victoria, who will work as a team to slice the Urfmine in long, even strips the width of your thumb so that they are long and narrow. I already have the potion brewing so when you're done slicing, give the pieces to me, and I will add them. We are making a small Midnight Potion. When you pour this potion on a particular patch of earth—up to a half of an acre—that whole section of the world will be pitch-black for about five minutes. We will use this tomorrow when we pick the Tengurin. Are you ready, pickers?"

"Yep," we answered.

"In 5, 4, 3, 2, 1," she said. And all of a sudden a blue and green vegetable burst from within the leaves. It looked like a round piece of corn, but the kernels were alternately blue, green, blue, green—as clear as the sky had been earlier in the day. I gently took a grip on the plant and pulled. It came off easy as pie. I handed it to Josh, who was nearest to me. I watched the six of them slice it and add it to the potion in no time. When it was sliced, it looked the same, with blue and green milky kernels. It was awesome though, because it looked like a neon, circular piece of corn, and it's not every day that you see one of those!

Soon the potion began bubbling and steaming. It was foul-smelling and pitch-black. Yep, it was *definitely* a Midnight Potion.

It seemed just a few moments since we had returned to our hotel room, but apparently it was already morning.

"Wake up, Ava and Victoria!" Professor Threcar said loudly. "We have a big day, and Poppy said we have to be at the green-house at 9:30. Hurry up!"

I opened my eyes and groggily, still half-asleep, walked into the bathroom, where I speed-showered and quickly fixed my hair. Then Victoria did the same and we were on our way to another day in the Sky Garden.

⚬⚬⚬❀⚬⚬⚬

The first thing we did in the greenhouse was put our leather gloves on. "Make sure… THEY'RE… NICE AND… TIGHT!" Professor Treeny sang. *Sniff, sniff.*

We made sure that our gloves were on securely so that nothing could reach our hands. We would have to water some plants with things that could scorch or burn our hands or even make them disappear.

"This is honey from our finest maple tree," Poppy announced proudly as she poured a quarter-cup of thick liquid into each of our watering cans. *What was she talking about? Maple trees didn't produce honey.* Then I thought, *Hey we're on Neptune. In the sky. On a floating garden. Anything goes here.*

"I would like you to honey-water our Dituniums with it, please. Use all of the honey on one plant. Do not be alarmed if it grows rapidly before your eyes. That's how it works here. We need to measure their growth, anyway, and this sort of speeds everything up."

I chose a large Ditunium, and, standing over it, poured the honey onto it. The Ditunium's width expanded about seven inches and it became extremely tall all of a sudden. How weird!

When we were done with the Dituniums, Poppy showed us her prize plant. "This is a Visidia," she exclaimed, bursting with pride. "It takes many months to grow, and it has to grow in different climates at crucial points in its life. Like, it needs snow in Month 4 and intense humidity in Month 8. That's why it has to grow in the greenhouse, because we can control the climate closely. Since these take so long to grow, they are *very* expensive. Their uses are either for spells, potions, or for very tasty dishes. But usually if you're using it in a food, you use only a very small part of it for flavor, because you want to make it last. As you can see, this one is at Month 6." I couldn't see this at all, but I guess she wasn't used to having many people here who didn't know about the plants.

"It has to have abundant rain all this month or it will not grow correctly. Now it *is* yellow, but tomorrow it may very well be a deep violet. You see, it alternates between those two colors, and nobody knows which it will be at the end of its growth. The plum color brings a better price, by the way.

"Any questions?"

There weren't, so we just kept watering plants with various liquids and helping her do odd jobs, like weed or pick out the dead leaves. We stopped for lunch at the main hall, and then continued in the greenhouse. Before we watered each plant, we received a lecture from either Professor Threcar, Professor

Treeny, or Poppy. By the end of the day, boy, I was ready to be back at Dream Ring.

We got to harvest a Tengurin, a bright turquoise plant that needed the Midnight Potion for harvest because it was so bright that if you looked directly at it, you would be blinded. The Midnight Potion dulled the glare and let us safely harvest the rare plant. That went right, and it was all good.

In the middle of one particularly long lecture from Professor Treeny, Professor Threcar looked at her watch. "Oh, look at the time!" she said quite loudly, causing Professor Treeny to stop his droning (and sniffing and stroking his goatee and, of course, the occasional song) and look up. "We really must get going. Students, thank Poppy for her helpful information about all these magical plants."

We thanked her numerous times and took one last look at the heavenly Sky Garden. Then we went through the boring, gray room and out the gates.

With a "Tar-Papa, Tar-Papa," we were back at the banana-shaped cloud where our brooms were stored, along with the rest of our luggage.

But someone else was there, too.

Chapter Thirty One

Waiting for me on the banana-shaped cloud was Widdi-dorm himself, the Evil Sorcerer. The one who destroys people without a second thought, who had been haunting me for much of my first year at Dream Ring.

"Ava Popolis. I will finish you today." His voice was small, wispy, but still powerful.

He wasn't much of a man. His form was see-through, not much more than a ghost. His hair was jet black, cut in a short buzz, and his eyes were full of hate, burning red with fury and anger. He wore black robes with a red cape, and he carried his wand.

It's sort of freaky to be at the opposite end of the greatest evil sorcerer in history's wand.

He laughed, menacing and terrifying. Then his eyes glowed with even more fire than before.

"I tried to kill you before. And, somehow, you escaped. I wonder how you escaped," he mused. But then he advanced on me growling, "NOBODY ESCAPES WIDDIDORM!" Then I remembered that we weren't alone. Everybody, even my teachers, were still with us, staring at us in shock. Widdidorm also realized that we had company.

"BLIND!" he screamed furiously, waving his wand, and my entire class fell down, unable to see. Then looking at me, he said "Papa-Tar Kapa-lavinia-parahna!" and then we were suddenly alone on Neptune, probably a few miles from the Lone Hotel. Thankfully, we were safely on the ground, so plummeting to my death was not a concern for me.

He grinned evilly. "Now that we're alone, I can finish you off properly." I was trembling, but my head was clear and I knew that it would take all my strength to survive this.

I racked my brain for spells that I could use in a sequence to get out. I could blind him; then I could get my broom back; then maybe I could blind him again and speed away. But he could likely defend against all my spells. I knew how to do a force field, but I could only hold it so long. And if I held it too long, then I would pass out, and he could just finish me off with a "slumber-iumptia." Probably best *not* to do the force field.

He tapped his wand against his black robes, as if trying to juice it up in order to get rid of me.

"Wingkapa!" he shouted, pronouncing it 'wing-kay-pah.' I quickly shrank until I was as tall as his knee. Luckily my wand was still normal-size, and I hit his foot with all of my force until he lifted his foot and whimpered.

"Wingkapa!" I shouted, and down he shrunk. He was still a little taller than me, naturally.

Then he used his wand as a stick, also, and started beating me. That's when I learned how *un-human* he is. He landed one hard blow of the wand to my leg. I heard a sickening crack and felt a jolt of pain. My vision blurred, and I swung wildly with my wand. I think I hit his head—he was see-through, but he was definitely there in body—because a few seconds later he was howling on the ground. I should've given him a good spell right then, but I was stupid. My shock gave him time to come back so he could finish me off.

Widdidorm made us both normal height again. It felt much better to be five-one than, like, two feet tall, but it made him look scarier at a towering height of, like, six-three.

He raised his wand above his head and hissed something that sounded like gibberish, but wasn't. A few seconds later a large object whirled around and hit the back of my head. I fell over, cradling my head in my arms. I couldn't see very well; the world was very blurry around the edges. I would've liked to curl up on the ground and just pass out, but I knew that would be the end of me. I wasn't ready for that.

So I clawed my way back up. Wracking my brain for spells, I yelled "SLUMBER-IUMPTIA!" as loud as I could. I felt a strong jolt from my wand, and I looked to see if Widdidorm was gone, but he wasn't. His white shield enveloped him, and through it I could see the anger and hate in his eyes intensify. I was in for it.

He did another spell I had never heard of, one which left me rooted to the ground. Uh-oh. I had planned on escaping after I brought my broom to me. I guess that wasn't happening.

I swayed with pain; my head was pulsing, and my leg was hurting so bad that I had to stand on one foot. "Wing-kah-pah!" I exclaimed weakly. Slowly Widdidorm began to rise into the air, a surprised look frozen on his face. I held my gaze and concentration with my wand until he was about fifty feet up. Then I purposely directed my attention elsewhere and he came crashing to the ground, howling with pain when he landed.

He was cut up and bruised just like me. But he was my mom's age, and he didn't lose the ability to do spells as quickly as I did. His body was already used to doing a lot of magic. I guessed that I only had two spells left, maybe three, before I passed out.

If I wanted to escape and possibly *kill* him, I would have to try one of the Slumber spells. I would have used my powers, but I wasn't sure yet *how* to use them. I would surely have to ask Professor Threcar for future reference.

"Hmmm… what was that spell for fire?" I wondered aloud. Widdidorm smirked at me, tapping his wand, probably thinking of a complicated spell that would affect me in some horribly painful way. I chose the moment when he was off-guard to do my spell. "SLUMBER-IUMPTIA!" I screamed with all the strength that I had left. Then for good measure, I said again, "SLUMBER-IUMPTIA!"

Widdidorm gave a loud scream shrill enough to rival the unhappiest newborn baby. He shrank down in pain, and his ghost-like form disappeared. I had a feeling he wasn't entirely in a coma—maybe just like a really deep sleep—but at least he was gone. I was safe for now.

With that thought, I finally passed out.

Chapter Thirty Two

I woke up in the hospital wing. My sight was a little blurry around the edges, and the world looked like it was black and white. I felt a sharp pain in my left leg, and looking down, I saw that it was in a gigantic white cast instead of the usual pain-fixer from Nurse Norah.

I only vaguely remember someone finding me a while after I passed out. He or she had carried me to the hospital wing, and then I had fallen into a deep sleep.

"Mom?" At least my voice still worked.

I heard a noise and looked to my left. It hurt my neck to move so suddenly, and for a second I thought I might pass out—again.

What I saw was my mother, crying and carrying on like I had come back from the dead.

"What are you crying about?"

She looked at me, shocked enough to stop crying. "Honey," she said. "You were this close"—she held her thumb and pointer finger about an inch apart—"to…" She broke down again. "To… d-d-d-d-dying."

I looked at her like she was crazy. Dying? I hadn't been close to *dying*.

Wait a minute… all of a sudden, my memory came flooding back to me. Widdidorm… spell-fight… miracle… pain. Yep. I *had* been close to dying.

And then the whole thing hit me. I started crying very hard. I had no energy, I was drained, and I was tired of being Widdi-dorm's target.

In the midst of my tears, I passed out again. I didn't even have enough energy to cry.

I was aware of someone covering me up with a soft flannel blanket and turning out the lights. Then I fell asleep for a long, long time.

When I woke up, I felt almost normal. My body wasn't, but my spirit felt a little more alive. My leg still felt like it was on fire, and I couldn't move without pain. But I was alive.

"Honey, how do you feel?" Mom asked from her chair beside my bed.

"Okay, I think," I answered weakly. "Better, anyway. Mom?" I croaked.

"Yes, dear?"

"What happened when my teachers and friends woke up and realized I was gone?"

"Oh, honey. They all looked for you, of course! When they couldn't find you, they flew straight here to Dream Ring and warned us. I had just arrived at Dream Ring, and I turned my flying carpet around in midair and flew off to look for you. We sent out another search party, too, and they found you." She wiped a few tears from her eyes, trying not to let her mascara or eyeliner run. "Ava, we need to talk."

"Yeah. Like, why was Widdidorm targeting me?" I asked.

"This is hard for me, so please be considerate."

"Sorry." I snuggled into my covers and waited for her story.

"Here goes.

"When I was at Dream Ring, I knew Widdidorm. His first name is Peter, and he was the most popular boy in school. He was so kind and caring. I personally knew him."

"You *knew* Widdidorm?"

"I did know Peter, yes. And James. Give me a minute."

"Sorry. Wait. Did you just say James. As in *Minaga*?"

"Yes. But that's not important. I dated Peter my third and fourth year."

"YOU *WHAT*?!"

"Yes. I dated Peter. We were best friends, and he was very romantic. We were Dream Ring's cutest couple for quite a long time.

"But Peter was from a troubled family. He had been at an orphanage because his dad was on drugs and his mom left, so he had never really known *family*. My family was the opposite. My mom was the sweetest little lady, and Dad was the most caring old man you could ever know.

"So one day, when we got to visit home, I took him with me. I was almost sixteen at the time, and I thought it would be good for him to meet my brothers and sisters, and especially my parents. Peter was quite excited to meet them, as he had heard much about them.

"While we were there my parents turned the charm on, even more than usual. They spoiled Peter for the week that he spent there, and he loved it. He was even kinder and more romantic to me when we went back to Dream Ring.

"But soon I noticed a change in him. Towards the end of our fourth year, he couldn't make most of our dates. He was still kind, but he had these *moods* where he was quite angry.

"So I broke up with him. It broke my heart because he was the sweetest man that I had ever known. But when he was angry, he was *dangerous*. And that scared me more than it hurt me to break up with him."

"Wow."

"There's more. Once I met your dad and married him, I realized something: Peter's anger was because of *my* family. It was a mistake to take him home with me. He was very angry because he realized that I had the better family in our relationship and it made him irrational. I don't know why, but he wanted revenge on me because he didn't have a loving family like me. It doesn't make much sense, but it's logical, in a way.

"And when he learned that I had a child coming to Dream Ring, he was determined to get revenge on me through you. He visited you in dreams and in all sorts of ways. Then he tried to hurt you, and miraculously, you resisted. He *will* try again, and I want you to be ready. So I have arranged with Professor Gophersmocker for spell-fight lessons for you in your second year. How does that sound?" She smiled for the first time, and I felt a little relief that the mood had been lifted a bit.

"Uh, good. I guess."

"Great. 'Cause you are already signed up for the lessons. It'll be good for you."

"Mom?"

"Yes?"

"I have one question."

"Ask away."

"How did Widdidorm know where I was and what time I would be leaving the Sky Garden?"

"Mr. Minaga gave you away. He had access to all the students' schedules."

"What's gonna happen to him?"

"Oh, he's already fired and in jail."

"Well, that's good."

"Some of your friends want to see you. Are you up for it?"

"Sure."

"I'll send 'em in."

A couple of minutes later, a group of my friends came in. Victoria, Kathryn, Ella, Tanya, Gabriella, Professor Threcar, and Mrs. Gophersmocker cautiously came into my room.

After making sure I was okay, my teachers stepped into another room to talk with Mom while I talked to my friends. Well, *they* talked to *me*. With all of their chattiness, I barely got a word in.

"Did you really meet him?"

"Did you kick his butt?"

"Omigosh. Are you okay?"

"What was he like?"

"Did you have a spell-fight?"

"What spells did you use?"

"How did you kick his butt?"

"How did you escape?"

"Is he dead?"

"Guys. Can I get a word in?" I asked weakly. I couldn't even tell who said what!

"Sorry," the group chorused sheepishly.

"Okay. Well, yes, I met Widdidorm. But not for the first time. He had really been wanting to harm me for a while now, so it was like the final verdict. Yes, Ella, I did kick his butt.

Sort of. I didn't cause him as much pain as he did to me, but I got out of it and he's gone for now. I don't exactly recall the details of what spells we used or how I escaped. I was in too much pain to think clearly, so I just said whatever came to mind."

"Oh. Wow."

"Are you okay?"

"Well, my leg is obviously broken. And I'm kind of beat up. He damaged my vision, but Nurse Norah said that it's not permanent and that she could fix it. I have a major migraine, and Nurse Norah says that my body is all 'spelled out' for a long time. Which is good, since we can't use magic 'til next August for the second year. And not being able to do spells makes the temptation of doing one during summer go away." I smiled weakly. "Kathryn, will you please adjust this bed so that I'm sitting up?"

She looked uncertain, but eventually figured out how to adjust my bed. "Thank you," I sighed. "Much more comfortable." She blew out a huge breath that lifted her curly brown bangs off her forehead.

"Okay, well, we better get going," Kathryn said. "Victoria can stay as long as you like, but Ella, Tanya, Gabriella and I still have to pack. Bye, Ava. I hope you feel better. See you in August!" They each attempted to give me a hug and then left.

"Has Nurse Norah told you how long it will be 'til I can get out of here?"

"Well, we're all leaving tomorrow, you know, since it's like almost the end of May. But Nurse Norah said that you can't get out of bed 'til mid-July. I'm sorry." Victoria gave me a look full of pity.

It hit me. *Mid-July. June. I had slept for over a week before waking up to reality.* "Really?" I squeaked.

"Yeah. To get out of Dream Ring we'll have you transported on a stretcher to the bed in the cellar of your broom. I'm gonna fly your broom home since I don't have one." I remembered that Victoria had to save her money and could maybe buy one in her second year.

"What am I going to do for *a month-and-a-half*?" I was getting hysterical. Panic was waking my body up and I felt like screaming. "I can't sit still that long!"

"Well, you could always write a book about your experiences here at Dream Ring," Victoria suggested.

"Yeah," I said, trying to calm down a little. Well, I could give it a try. I mean, I *had* had a lot of experiences here at Dream Ring. It might be a good book, actually.

Victoria stayed a lot longer, but eventually she had to go. "Bye. I'll see you on Friday. Well, tomorrow."

"Bye."

When she left, I stayed awake for a long time. I mean, the whole thought that Mom sort of caused Peter to turn into evil Widdidorm is kinda creepy. When she said that we "need to talk," I had imagined a totally different conversation (I don't know why, but I did). I was surprised and sort of scared. I mean, she had said that Widdidorm would try to kill me again. I just hoped that next time I would be ready.

"Goodbye!" we called to all of the teachers standing on the front steps of Dream Ring, at the entrance to the main hall. "See you next year!"

The jailers had brought Mr. Minaga from his jail cell so that we could glare at him as we walked by to our brooms or mobiles. When I was carried out on my stretcher, I gave him an extra-hard glare, and I didn't even feel tired. He looked like he would burst into tears when he saw that I was still alive and well. That made me smile sweetly at him and say, "Have a nice summer in jail, Mr. Minaga." Mom quickly shushed me and admonished me for talking so rudely to a teacher, which I didn't mind at all.

Once we were on the way back to Earth, I bounced between thinking about my proposed book and napping. I thought it was shaping up to be a pretty good book...

Want more of the story?

LOOK FOR BOOK 2 IN SPRING OF 2012!

WIDDIDORM:
Book 2 in the Dream Ring Series

Ava and Victoria are back at Dream Ring for their second year. Ava plans secret trips on Neptune, some resulting in more trouble than others! When Widdidorm puts more pressure than ever on Ava, she and Victoria embark on a journey through space and find themselves in a battle for survival. Will they both make it back to Neptune?